NINE LIVES

BERNICE RUBENS

Nine Lives

LITTLE, BROWN

A *Little, Brown* Book

First published in Great Britain by Little, Brown in 2002

Copyright © Bernice Rubens 2002

The moral right of the author has been asserted.

A CIP catalogue record for this book is available
from the British Library.

ISBN 0 316 85911 7

Typeset in Galliard by Palimpsest Book Production Limited,
Polmont, Stirlingshire
Printed and bound in Great Britain by
Clays Ltd, St Ives plc

Little, Brown
An imprint of Time Warner Books UK
Brettenham House
Lancaster Place
London WC2E 7EN

www.TimeWarnerBooks.co.uk

For Shaz and Rebecca

'Name?' the warder asked.
'Dorricks.'

'Mrs? Miss? Or Ms?' His eyebrow sneered.

'Mrs,' I said, and I wondered how and why I had attained such a status.

'Christian name?' The warder was thorough.

'Verine?' I said. I posed it as a question, because I was not sure if it would do.

He wrote down the names in order of unimportance. There was no doubt about the Dorricks or the Mrs. It was the Verine bit that was the problem. I never knew where the accent lay. So when I announced it, I gave equal stress to both syllables, *Ver-ine*, because I was loath to sell myself short. That's been my trouble all my life. Not knowing how I'm pronounced. My parents called me Verry, which gave no clue at all. That's my problem. I think it acounts for all my troubles. I cannot give myself an accurate label. Even my husband, Mr Dorricks, calls me Verry. Such a silly name, considering there's very little 'very' about me. I'm a half-hearted woman. My feelings were stunted at birth and never dared go the whole way. I am irresolute, timorous, shuffling and pliant and have been all my life. I looked after my sons' welfare but it was Mr Dorricks who arranged their education, their leisure and their future prospects. I complied. It was Mr Dorricks who dictated my wardrobe and I obeyed. Mr Dorricks ruled the roost and I accepted it, unwilling to explore alternatives. Nothing 'very' about all that. He might as well have called me 'Ginger', solid brunette that I am.

'Down the corridor. First on the left,' the warder said. I took myself fearfully down the passageway, that half-hearted self of mine, my steps without purpose, except to get the visit over and done with, not knowing what to say, or how to say it. Whether to collude or question, to agree or object, or simply to nod or shake my head, donating to approval or rejection a cowardly ambiguity.

'Hello Donald,' I rehearsed but I could go no further. I wasn't going to say 'How are you?' because he might tell me and then I would have to accommodate his answer and give him sympathy or grounds for hope. But between you and me, I couldn't stretch to either. Because I didn't know what I believed. I just knew that I loved him – of that I was sure. But it was that very certainty that nagged at me, for, after all that had happened, how could I insist on loving him? Then I recalled how affectionately he had cared for me over the years, how wonderful a father he had been to our two boys. So despite the verdict, even if it was just, and I wasn't too sure about that, how could I *not* love him? My feelings simply bewildered me.

He was alone in the room, undeniably visible, so that I was allowed no time to try to locate him. He stood up when he saw me and stretched out his hand. I was disturbed by what looked like a sign of welcome, a plea for sympathy and understanding. I took his proffered hand, and I wondered with horror where it had been and what it had been up to. Then I quickly took a seat to distance myself.

'I'm innocent, you know,' he said, before I had even time to sit down. 'You know that, don't you?' He almost threatened me.

'Yes,' I said, because I had to. How else could I validate the many years that I had shared his bed?

'How are you?' I asked, not meaning to. Not meaning to say anything at all.

He began to tell me and I tried not to listen. But I heard the fury in his voice, the pleading, the blame, the villification of all those who had accused him and, above all, his enraged declaration of innocence. I heard every syllable of it, but I didn't listen. Occasionally I nodded or shook my head, expressing nothing at all, as if my puppeteer had gone off for a short break and left two random strings in operation. All through his recital, I was looking at him, but I can't recall seeing him.

'I love you Verry,' I heard him say.

I was stunned. Never in all our years together had he so declared himself. I did not doubt his sincerity, but I marvelled at his sudden outspokenness. He had always been so tight-lipped, so reticent; it was as if he stood naked before me. I was embarrassed yet moved.

'I love you too, Donald,' I said. I would not deal further with that subject so I quickly talked about life outside the prison, items of news, the goings-on in our street. I lied about them, because most of the goings-on centred around Donald's crimes and conviction. I talked about the weather, boring myself, and not knowing what I was saying, anxious for my visiting time to be over and done with, yet wary of my freedom in the streets where I would have to wonder what I ought to be feeling. I held Donald's hand, as much for my own safety as for his, then I heard a recorded voice calling 'time's up', and I sighed with relief.

I rose. He tightened his grip on my hand. 'Believe me, Verry,' I heard him say. 'Verry, Verry, you have to believe me.'

It was at that moment I decided to change my name. I

smiled at him, or rather to myself, pleased with my decision. I eased my shoulders out of his grip, smiling all the while.

'See you,' I said, and quickly left the room.

I strutted my way out of the prison. No longer Verry, that lie of a name. I am Joan now, I decided. No accent problems with that one. Joan Dorricks I am, I said to myself. The Dorricks bit I would deal with later. Perhaps that label too would have to be replaced.

I wanted to meet someone who would ask me my name just so I could try it out on someone other than myself. I was passing a doctor's surgery, and on an impulse I went inside. The waiting room was crowded, but it would not affect my purpose. I approached the receptionist.

'I have an appointment,' I heard myself say.

'Name please?' the woman asked.

'Joan,' I said. 'Joan Dorricks.' I loved its echo and cadence. Then I left hurriedly as the woman was vainly searching through the appointments book.

It sounded real enough, I thought on the bus-ride home and I repeated it to myself, sometimes loudly, so that the other passengers looked at me with pity. And then I began to dislike the name and to see no purpose in using it. 'Verry,' I said aloud and I confess I felt suddenly at home with it, though that home had become a place of such horror and misery.

Mrs Thomas, my neighbour, was weeding her front garden as I reached my house. A semi-detached house, though not on the Thomas side, which allowed for over-the-fence conversation.

'How is he?' Mrs Thomas asked.

'Fine,' I said. It was a good response in that it couldn't

be questioned. 'Fine' was an absolute term, unlike 'bearing up' or 'very low', phrases which begged analysis and, worst of all, understanding. And that was the last thing I wanted. I didn't like Mrs Thomas very much. The woman was after tittle-tattle. She had already profited by her status as the 'monster's neighbour'. 'Such a mild-looking man,' she told the newspapers. 'Wouldn't hurt a fly,' was the phrase she used on television. Now she would have nothing to report except that, according to his wife, the prisoner was fine, and 'fine' didn't sell newspapers. 'Fine' was a disappointing word.

I hurried up the path, pulling my house key out of my bag. I was anxious to be alone. I needed a board meeting with myself, though from long practice I knew it would come to nothing. As I expected, there was no one in the house, but even after all these months of emptiness its vacancy still surprised me.

On the day that Donald had been sentenced, my two children had made arrangements to leave home. I still think of them as children, though neither of them will see twenty again. Twins they are. Matthew and Martin. They were a surprise. There are no twins in my family. Nor in Donald's. At least, not as far as I know, but I know little about his family. Next to nothing, in fact. He has never talked about them and I've always been afraid to ask. But they're lovely, my boys, and very close to each other. What one does, the other will follow. I did not blame them for going. To tell the truth, I envied them, for their departure made it clear that they had no doubts about the verdict, though I could have done with their assistance, but I know it would have been a false support which in time would have crumbled under its own deception.

I made myself a pot of tea. Two teabags, and one for the pot. As far as I was concerned, my whole family was still at home. Nothing had changed. Donald was walking the dog, and the boys were out with their friends. But when night came, I had to face the still empty house and the board meeting that had come to naught. I thought of going to bed, but I knew that I would not sleep, but would count the days to the time of my next obliged visit. Donald's lawyers, the ones he sacked, had advised me to move to another town, far away and, once there, to revert to my maiden name. I loved that word 'maiden'. It branded me innocent. But such a move would confirm Donald's guilt, and I couldn't let him down. In any case, he had told me he was innocent, and in all our years together I had never known him to lie. And now I began to share his anger with his accusers and their preposterous conclusions. I cleared the table of its four cups and saucers, and the teapot, still almost full, and I decided that my family would be late home. I would not wait up for them. I would go to my bed.

Before they took Donald away, I used to look forward to bedtime. He was a great cuddler, my Donald. Warm and cosy, and we fitted together very nicely. But now, since his arrest, I toss and I turn and try to work out what happened. And try not to, at the same time, in case I stumble on something that doesn't make sense – that maybe points to his guilt – and then I try to stop thinking, which isn't easy if you can't get off to sleep. I am so confused. I wish somebody else could tell me what had happened. And why. Somebody will tell it anyway. Writers probably. They'll get it all right, and they'll get it all wrong. But they won't get to the truth, because only I, I, Verry Dorricks, know it.

Fairly and squarely. Yet, at the same time, I don't know it because I cannot face it.

So let the writers have a go. No one's going to stop them trying. But none of them is inside Donald, and none of them is inside me. But let them write what they will. The truth has many faces. One need not confront them all.

EXCERPT FROM THE DIARY OF
DONALD DORRICKS

ONE DOWN. EIGHT TO GO.

The first was the hardest. I expected that. Nothing to do with conscience or scruple. I have no qualms. It's a question of practice, I suppose. The next ones should be easier.

I was meticulous in my preparations. I rang the United Kingdom Council for Psychotherapy, and I told them that I needed help. I gave a false name, of course, and affected a Scottish accent. But I told them I lived in London. I am not adventurous. London is big enough for anonymity. They told me where I could acquire a list of practitioners and it was up to me to choose someone in my area. They did not ask for my address, for which I was grateful. I studied the list in the privacy of my office. It covered practitioners over the whole country. I settled on a group from the outer suburbs, far away from where I lived. Then I shut my eyes and stuck a pin into the list. It landed on one called Harry Winston. Poor bugger. But whatever he was called, he would do for starters. I rang him forthwith and made an appointment for the following Monday, giving him the name and accent I had used for the Council.

Mr Winston had a kindly voice, and I did not thank him for it. I would have preferred a gruff and grudging tone, as if he were doing me a favour. I tried to ignore it. His kindness would get him nowhere.

I had long considered disguises, and I kept the basics in my office. It was there that I stuck on a beard, and donned a trilby hat, in which I looked frankly ridiculous. And the gloves. Most important, the gloves. I'd bought a few pairs in different colours. And then my weapon, unseen in my pocket.

I drove to Mr Winston's house, but I parked my car a few streets away. I noticed that there were few people about, it being a quiet residential area, and those few who walked the streets did not worry me. I was confident in my disguise. I carried the gloves but I did not put them on until I faced his front door. There were two bells on the panel, and I pressed the one that claimed 'Consultant'.

'Who is it?' came through the voice grid.

I announced myself and was ordered to the first floor. The door opened and I went through. I was suddenly nervous and I felt sweat on my forehead. As I climbed the stairs, a shadow fell across the landing, and when I reached the top, sweating and shivering, I knew I looked like a suitable case for treatment.

Mr Winston stepped into the shadow and welcomed me. I wished he had been less of a gentleman.

'Come in,' he said. 'Sit down. Take off your things. It's a hot day.'

'Not the gloves,' I said. 'Never the gloves. That's why I'm here, you see.' I had done my homework. I knew about glove fetishism.

'As you wish,' Mr Winston said. He was smiling, clearly looking forward to a field day. He sat down at his desk.

The sweat was pouring from me now. I felt it dripping down my neck. It was too late to withdraw. I had to finish the job in hand. But his smile unnerved me and, in any case, I would welcome a delay. So I rattled on about the gloves.

'I wear them all the time,' I said. 'Can't take them off. I don't control them. They're like glove puppets and someone else is pulling the strings.' I was rather pleased with my little invention and I smiled at him.

'Someone else is in control, you say? Is that how you feel about them?'

'That's right,' I said. I could sense that I'd opened a can of worms and that I had pleased him with the clue I had offered as to which direction he should take. But as far as I was concerned, he wasn't going anywhere, despite my signposting. Yet I was loath to get on with the job. It was fear that delayed me, I confess, and a little curiosity as to how he would exploit my clue.

'Tell me when and where it began, when you were first aware of this control,' he said.

Well, frankly, I couldn't be bothered and, in any case, I'd run out of invention. So I crossed to his desk and took the guitar-string out of my pocket. My hands were trembling.

Mr Winston half rose. 'What are you doing?' he asked.

I think he was suddenly afraid. I quickly placed myself behind him and forced him to sit.

'Go away, go away,' he said. 'You're out of your mind.'

I was able to hate him then, and it was easy to circle his neck with my string. I was not out of my mind. I was not even beside my mind. I had never felt so sane. I stood well back so that his blood could not stain me – I had rehearsed my movements often enough – and I pulled the string tight. He gurgled. I had hit the spot. I watched as the blood ran down his waistcoat and his head fell forward. Then he was still. With my gloved hand on his neck, I checked for a pulse. He was gone.

And so was I. Swiftly down the stairs and out the way I came. As I walked towards my car, I began to shiver. The sweat still poured from me, but I was cold. I passed a group of schoolboys, too busy with their quarrelling to notice me. I was tempted to run, but that might have drawn someone's attention. My car seemed a million miles away. Once there, I sank into the seat, breathless, and I started to drive straight away, unwilling to give myself time to think. The next one will be easier, I told myself. And the next. And so on until I have completed my mission. I kept reminding myself of the whys and the wherefores I had become a murderer. The reason, the motive, all that made me feel a little better. By the time I reached my office, I was myself again.

ONE DOWN. EIGHT TO GO.

Mrs Penny Winston was a primary-school teacher, and every Monday she was free after three o'clock. Her boys would not be home from school until five, so she had time to do the week's shopping. It was her Monday routine. She trundled her trolley around the supermarket, and she considered herself a happy woman. Two well-adjusted sons, Paul and James, diligently at work for their exams. Soon both of them would be at university and would probably have left home. And then there would be just herself and Harry and she looked forward to that, for their partnership was a solid one that over the years had grown in affection and respect. 'I'm a lucky woman,' she said to herself, and tried not to feel smug.

The boys were home from school when she returned and they helped her offload the shopping. She set about preparing supper. Harry's last patient would be gone by seven. Then he would come downstairs and join her in a pre-prandial cocktail. A martini. Every evening at seven. The boys went to the nearby park to play tennis, also part of the routine but they would return in time for supper and home-work thereafter. I run a tight ship, Penny thought, a little disturbed by her own conceit. Such ideas tempted the gods and the evil eye. But all that was nonsense, she told herself, as she liquidised the broccoli soup for their first course.

Shortly before seven, the boys returned and set to laying the table. Meanwhile, Penny prepared the cocktails and set the tray on the drawing-room side-table. A small bowl of nuts completed the picture, as the church clock struck seven.

Penny sat down and waited. She listened for Harry's tread on the stairs, and was faintly unnerved by the sudden silence in the house. She couldn't understand it. Every evening at seven, Harry's footsteps chimed with the church bell. He was meticulous in his timing. His last patient must surely have left by now. Yet she was reluctant to call him. He was possibly catching up with paperwork and it was an unspoken rule in the house that he was never to be disturbed. She waited until seven-fifteen, then she poured herself a martini to steady her nerves. Paul and James crept into the drawing room. Why this tip-toeing, she wondered. And why this terrible silence?

'Where's Dad?' James whispered. 'He's late.'

Which indeed he was, and would never be later. They held on to the silence until seven-thirty. And then Penny said something that in future she would live endlessly to regret and would forever punish herself for the damage she had caused to her deeply loved sons.

'Go and see what he's up to, James,' she said.

'Why me?' James asked. He knew his father's rule of privacy.

'I'll go,' Paul said. 'If you come with me.' It was as if he was volunteering for the dark and was frightened.

'Fair enough,' James said, and they crept up the stairs, dodging each other, neither of them willing to go first.

They arrived together at their father's door. And together they knocked. And waited. After a little while, they knocked again.

'He's not there,' James said, anxious to make a hasty retreat. 'He must have gone out.'

'I'm going to open it and see,' Paul said. 'You're coming in with me. Dad?' he called out, giving him a last chance to respond. So they opened the door to break the silence.

Downstairs, Penny heard the screaming. Later on she would wonder why she didn't respond immediately, why she took time to finish her martini and even to nibble a few nuts. As she stood up, her knees melted, and she hobbled to the staircase. 'I'm coming,' she said, and she didn't recognise her own voice.

The boys stood in the doorway.

'Don't go in,' James whimpered. 'It's terrible.'

But she pushed past them and greeted the scene in dumbfounded silence. She crossed over to his desk and stroked his hair.

'Don't touch anything,' Paul said. 'We must call the police.'

She went on stroking as the tears rolled down her cheeks. She was tempted to lift his head, but she dreaded what she would find. The boys put their arms around her and led her away. Their oh-so-bright futures were blighted and they would need someone of their father's calling to comfort them. Or not. One who would, according to his or her personal hang-ups, presume they thought of themselves as killers, and would go the long road over many years to convince them that they had not murdered their father, when such a thought had never crossed their minds in the first place. Such a technique could also pass as comfort, but God knows to what horrendous ends.

The boys brought their mother back to the drawing room. Paul poured her another drink while James went into the hall to phone the police. The door was open, so his message could be heard. 'Come quickly,' he whimpered. 'Our father's dead.' He included Paul in his loss. 'Murdered,' he said, after a pause, and in one muffled syllable. 'Come quickly,' he said again, as if their speed

might resuscitate his father. He gave the address nonchalantly as if, compared to his loss, its location was irrelevant.
Then he returned to the drawing room. Paul was drinking
the second martini as though he'd already replaced his
father.

The police came quickly and discreetly. Just two of them
at first. In plain clothes, and in an unmarked car. Not sufficient cause to merit the raising of net curtains in the close.
James opened the door for them and motioned them up
the stairs. He was reluctant to lead them, but they found
their way.

The door to Harry's consulting room was wide open.
Aghast.

Downstairs, the family could find no words. It was too
soon for speculation, too soon even for anger. The time
was ripe only for disbelief. And silence. A silence sometimes
broken by footsteps overhead and the sudden ringing of
the doorbell. Then hasty footsteps down the stairs, and the
opening of the front door and the tread of several feet to
the first landing. Paul poured his mother another martini
and one for himself. This was not routine. There would be
no seven o'clock supper tonight. There would be no home-
work after the uneaten meal. Routine was shattered and
their lives would never be the same again. And still the
silence and bewilderment that could not find words. Broken
at last by a knock on the door.

It was a policeman. 'My name is Detective Inspector
Wilkins,' he said as he entered. 'I am very sorry.' How often
had he used that phrase, he wondered. And did he still
mean it after all its frequency? But in this case, children
were involved and he meant it well enough, for how could
they survive such a horrendous legacy?

'How did he die?' Penny had at last found her voice. Wilkins had dreaded that question, for its true answer would in no way ease her sorrow.

'Strangled,' he said. It was a half-truth. But 'garrotted' was unpronounceable and smacked of medieval cruelty. 'Death was immediate,' he said. 'He didn't suffer.' Another phrase he had used often enough and never been too sure of its truth. But true or not, it was standard procedure.

'The pathologist hazards the death at four o'clock. Was anybody at home at that time?'

They shook their heads.

'I was at the supermarket,' Penny said. 'And the boys were at school.'

'We've looked at your husband's diary,' Wilkins said. 'His last patient at four o'clock was a Mr George Pendry. No address is given. Do you know that name, Mrs Winston?' he asked

'No,' Penny said. 'I had little to do with my husband's profession. It is one of confidentiality, you know.'

'I understand,' Wilkins said. There would be little help from that quarter, he knew, and that oath of secrecy in the profession could hinder his investigation further. He had more questions to ask, but he sensed that this was no time for investigation. 'We have to remove your husband's body,' he said. 'We shall do a post-mortem.'

It was that word that brought the truth to the three of them. Disbelief dispersed and together they began to weep, holding each other in their sorrow.

'I'm sorry,' Wilkins said again. He backed towards the door. 'I'll be in touch. We'll find whoever did it,' he said. 'I promise you.'

But he knew he was in no position to make such a

promise. There were no fingerprints, no signs of a break-in. No disturbance. Only a body with a guitar string around its neck. He shuddered as he recalled it. Garrotting was rare, and never left clues. It was a distant manoeuvre. Safe. A non-touching crime, executed from behind. Gruesome. He opened the front door and took a gulp of fresh air. He would wait for the ambulance to arrive. When it came, sidling slowly into the kerb, the net curtains found a cause, and all over the close they were raised in curiosity tinged with pleasure. There was no movement around the vehicle. It looked patient, parked there, un-urgent, which indeed it was, for the dead were in no hurry. The neighbours waited too, and were shortly rewarded with the sight of two men with a stretcher who alighted from the van and went to open the back doors. And, what's more, to carry the stretcher between them, which they took into the house. The neighbours waited and shortly the stretcher reappeared, covered with a black cloth. Then it was loaded into the van, which drove away as silently as it had arrived. The show was over, but they had only viewed the final act. In time, they would learn of the drama behind the scenes.

The neighbourhood was appalled. Harry Winston was a loved man in the community. A generous man, an organiser of good causes, a wonderful husband and father. This almost-too-good-to-be-true reputation served to feed the anger and indignation of his many friends. Even his patients, who came forward willingly to testify to his compassion and skill. According to the Council for Psychotherapy, Harry Winston was a leading pioneer in the field. His killer had to be found. And quickly.

DI Wilkins did his best, but he had little to go on. Few

witnesses could be traced, apart from a couple of school-boys who said that they had seen a man walking past them at around that time. But they couldn't remember what he looked like, except for his trilby hat which they thought was a bit 'square'. But that man could have been anybody. No one could be found who bore Mr Winston a grudge though Wilkins trailed through his list of patients, past and present, some dead, but others alive enough to praise him. The press was on his back, as was his superior, as well as the mayor of the borough who accused him of dragging his feet. Mr Harry Winston would not be put on the back-burner. What promised to be but a nine-days' wonder stub-bornly persisted through the coming weeks, but eventually indignation waned. There were lives to be lived and a future to face. All that was left was sympathy and support for the widow and her children.

But at headquarters, the file was kept doggedly open. DI Wilkins, desperate for leads, organised a reconstruction of the crime on *Crimewatch*, but never, in the long history of that series, had there been so little feedback. Wilkins sensed that the killer would strike again. And possibly in the same manner. He would bide his time. And his faith was not misplaced.

I slept very badly last night. Always do before I have to go and see Donald. He's been moved. Much further away. Maximum security, they call it, as if they expect him to escape. I have to laugh. My Donald escaping. He's far too lazy even to think about it. Always has been. Especially since the legacy. An uncle of his, no children, left him a packet – enough for him to give up work. He was tempted, but I dissuaded him. I didn't want him around the house all day. Still, he didn't work much. He must have been the laziest accountant in London. He kept his office, but he didn't employ a secretary. He sat there all alone, doing the books. Bit of a loner, my Donald. He'll not be unhappy in solitary.

It was a long journey. I had to change trains twice and then get a bus at the other end. Still, it didn't matter. It gave me time to think. Think about what I was going to say to him. But we never talked much, even when he was free. In all our years of marriage, I know no more about him now than when we first met. He never talked about his family. I didn't even know if he had any brothers or sisters. Or if his parents were still alive. He went to a funeral once, a few years ago, but he didn't mention whose it was. Maybe his dad or his mum. There was another funeral shortly after that one, so I presumed he was an orphan. He didn't seem too upset about either of them. When we first met, I thought he'd introduce me to his family, but he said they were always travelling, mostly abroad. But he promised that he'd get us together one day.

I never reminded him of that promise. I thought it might upset him. I took him to meet mine though, just my mum, because my father had left, and she quite took to Donald. She's dead now too. I'm glad she didn't live to see what happened. But I miss her. I could do with her advice at this time. Or some explanation, because I don't understand it at all.

The first train journey was a short one. Just two stops, so there was no point in settling my mind to thinking. I would wait till I got on the next train. An hour's journey that one, and plenty of time to wonder what to say to him. Whatever I do say to him. I didn't know if it was the truth or a lie – whether he really did what they all said he did. Surely I would have noticed? If a man murders ten people, surely his wife would notice some change in his behaviour? He would have been nervous, ill-tempered and terrified. But not my Donald. On the contrary, he was elated sometimes, really cheerful, as if he'd pulled off some big business deal. And on some nights, just between you and me, he made love just like Casanova. Though I don't know who Casanova was, but I've heard it said he was a great lover. Of course we made love from time to time, just matter-of-fact stuff, but those times I'm talking about, those special times, he seemed possessed. I enjoyed those thoughts on my train journey and I indulged in them, all the way to the prison. So that when I arrived, I still had no idea what I was going to say to him.

This was my first visit to the new prison, so I had to make myself known all over again, with that same name that I don't know how to pronounce.

'*Ver-ine*,' I said, giving each syllable an equal chance. The warder looked at me as if I were lying. 'Dorricks will do,' he said. 'Through the swing doors on your left.'

I made my way to reception, and felt like a new prisoner. I was led into a long corridor lined with booths. I had to sit facing a glass partition and wait for Donald to appear behind it.

'Use the phone to talk,' the warder said, acknowledging me as a first-timer. 'You'll get used to it.'

I'll have plenty of time to accustom myself, I thought. Donald was in for life. But would I keep visiting him, month after month, dissembling on a telephone line? Or would I cut my losses? Take the advice of Donald's lawyer and move to another place? But I'd only do that if I was convinced my Donald was a murderer. And personally, I don't have any proof.

I waited for Donald to appear, and when he did, shortly afterwards, I was struck by how well he looked. Prison suited him. He'd put on a little weight and though his hair was closely shaven, he looked a lot younger. An innocent face, I thought, a claim that he confirmed immediately as he picked up the phone.

'I'm innocent,' he said, as he always did. 'You believe that, don't you?'

I nodded into the phone.

He pressed his hand over the partition and I sensed that I had to cover it with my own. He smiled and so did I. I loved that glass wall. It meant he couldn't embrace me or touch me in any way. All he could savour was the print of my hand, as lustful as a kiss through a wooden panel. But there was more to the glass than the distance it entailed. Much more. It gave me a sudden sense of freedom. I was untouchable, so I could say anything I wanted. All the questions I'd been too timid to ask in our many years together could now be released without fear of irritated response.

'D'you have any other visitors?' I dared to ask. 'Your parents?' He shook his head over the phone.

'Dead,' he said. 'Both of them.' It had taken all those years of co-habitation, and a glass partition, to inform me that my husband was an orphan.

'Any brothers? Sisters?' I was becoming bold.

'No. I'm an only,' he said.

At last he had spoken. That mouth of his, that after almost thirty years of marriage had been clammed shut on such basic information, had now, with the shield of a glass partition, suddenly opened. It was not so much the news itself that astonished me; it was the realisation that I had been so accepting of his silence and for so long – that I had never questioned his reserve, his reticence. I had simply acknowledged him as a dark horse. Yet I thought I knew him, and knew him well, but now I understood that I knew nothing of the *core* of him and I had made do with his simple outline.

'You must have been lonely as a child,' I said.

He shrugged. 'I don't want to talk about it.'

The glass partition clearly prescribed limits. But I would not stop trying to make him out. I would persist, I decided. Next time, I'd visit him as long as I needed. As long as I needed to ferret out the nub of him and perhaps begin to fathom what was, until now, beyond my understanding. Through a glass darkly, I would begin to unravel my doubts.

'I would like to see the boys,' he said.

I had no answer to that one. They had written him off and he was unlikely to see them ever again.

22

'They think I'm guilty, don't they?' he said.

Again I had no answer. They, and the twelve jurors, good and true, I thought, along with thousands of others. What was so odd about me that I couldn't go along with the majority verdict? I suppose it was pride. For how could I admit to having lived with and loved such a man? It was vanity, the flipside of my self-contempt. But I would persevere. I would come again and again. At the end of that telephone line, I would wrench out of him all that he was loath to tell me. I would wring him dry.

'You don't have to come if you don't want to,' he said.

At that moment, I could have shattered the glass and put my arms around him. I don't know whether it would have been a gesture of love, or perhaps pity. Probably, alas, the latter. For pity is so hard to live with. It diminishes both parties. It would have been easier to hate him. Or to love him even. Either of those feelings I could live with and learn from. But pity corrodes, and my nights were sleepless enough without it.

'I haven't heard from the boys myself,' I said into the phone. I wanted to be part of his isolation.

'You must be lonely,' he said.

'Yes. I miss you.' And I meant it.

'Me too,' he said. And smiled.

I couldn't think of anything more to say, and I was relieved when the warder appeared and put his hand on Donald's shoulder. It seemed a gentle touch and I was grateful for it.

'Time's up,' he said.

Donald took his hand from the glass, and mine was left there, reprinting nothing. I watched him leave. He did not look behind him, so there was no point in waving. But I kept my hand on the partition, as if to reserve that spot as my own. Because I would be coming back; and back again until I could prise the truth out of him, so that I could cease to be ashamed of my ignorance.

THE DIARY

TWO DOWN. SEVEN TO GO.

It's six months now since poor Harry Winston, and I reckon the trail has run cold. I was lucky because I took risks. I didn't know that he was married, and had children. Any of them could have been in the house. But you live and learn. From now on, I will choose loners, and check out their joints beforehand.

Once more to my list and my choice fell on a Miss Angela Mayling who lived in Birmingham. It did no harm to widen my net. I told Verry I had business in Devon. Then I drove in the opposite direction to investigate my quarry. There was a coffee shop on the corner, and her house was obliquely opposite. I sat myself by the window and ordered lunch. That gave me a legitimate hour's stay. During that time, I saw a man ring her bell and a woman, who I presumed was my next target, answered the door and let him in. As I was finishing my dessert, I spotted the man leaving and I assumed he was a patient. As I was paying my bill, a woman was seen to ring her bell. She too was greeted by my quarry and invited to enter. I didn't hang around any longer − it would have risked being spotted and recalled. I decided to wait a good two months before striking again, so that any possible witness of my visit that day would have well and truly forgotten all about me. After a decent interval, I told Verry that I had to go to Devon again. My Verry doesn't question anything, which is just as well. She just accepts what I tell her, and gets on with it.

I invented a new name for myself and I rang Miss Mayling

for an appointment. Seven o'clock in the morning was all she could offer me. Such an hour indicated an overnight stay, but I couldn't risk a hotel. So I left London very early and drove through the breaking dawn to the site of my target. Once parked, I put on my gloves and a bowler hat. I liked to ring the changes. There was no one about; unsurprising at that hour. I was not sweating this time. Nor was I afraid. Once convinced of one's mission, there is no place for fear. I rang her bell without hesitation and, as expected, she answered the door.

'Miss Mayling?' I asked. I did not bother to disguise my voice – she would never live to identify it. She invited me inside, and as I entered I took out my string. Then I swept behind her, necklaced her throat and viciously pulled. She fell backwards on to the tiled floor of the hall. The blood spurted, and her pulse was still. Then I was out of the door, and into the empty street and my patient and innocent car for the return journey. For some reason, I was out of breath, as if I had been running. Yet I had walked calmly to her home, and with equal calm dispatched her. But my heart was racing. I started the car, for I daren't linger in fear of witnesses, and by the time I was out of the city I was calm again. And elated. I could not tell my Verry what I had done, but I would give her a good seeing-to with my new-found passion.

TWO DOWN. SEVEN TO GO.

The church clock was striking eight as Neil Clarkson turned into Shepton Road. She lived at the end of the street, so he would be late. At least two minutes late and she would dock it off his time. Money-grubbing bitch, he thought. At eight o'clock in the morning, three times a week, every week for the past six years, he had rung her bell and winced at the echo of the nursery chimes. Three times a week, each week, for the past six years and every bell ring at thirty quid a throw. He hated her. Though once, years ago, he remembered, he had loved her. 'Transference,' they called it. But that mercifully was short-lived. More than once he had tried to get rid of her. But she had a hold on him, in a grip that tightened over the years. Sometimes he felt that she needed him more than he did her.

He opened her gate and pressed viciously on the bell. He waited, offended by the chimes. Normally, if that were a word that could be applied to her profession, she would open the door as the chimes still echoed. But there was no response. He looked at his watch and he waited. After three minutes, he reckoned she owed *him*, so he rang again and kept his finger on the buzzer. The chimes of 'Baa, baa, black sheep' rang out over the neighbourhood in monotonous repetition.

Next door, a woman appeared at an upstairs window. 'Stop that racket,' she yelled, and she slammed the window down as the sheep bleated for the last time.

Neil Clarkson waited. He was afraid to ring the bell again. The door sported a wide letter box. He hesitated before

27

lifting the flap. She might catch him, and he knew she over-valued her privacy. But he would risk it. He looked around. There wasn't a soul on the street, and the woman at the window had no doubt gone back to bed. Gingerly he lifted the flap so that it was only half ajar. But it was wide enough to stun him. He dropped the flap in panic. Even through that narrow aperture, it was clear that she was dead. He thought it might be wishful thinking on his part, so he looked again, this time lifting the flap to its limit. And there indeed she lay, spread-eagled on the floor and laced in blood. He dropped the flap again and wondered what to do. But first he had to deal with the extraordinary feeling of relief that overcame him. Of bliss almost. At last he was shot of her. No longer did he have to grapple week after week with his broken relationship with his father. It was *his* father, and he could feel what he wanted about him. It was none of her business. And never had been. She had tried to divert him from blame, but over the years she had cunningly nurtured that blame in order to keep him by her. For the first time in so many years, Neil Clarkson felt free and with only a slight nudge of shame, he celebrated her passing.

But he couldn't leave her lying there. She deserved to be reported. He needed a phone. He would call next door, he thought, but not the side of the rattling window. The other side might be more welcoming. He pressed the door-bell and was rewarded with an 'Oranges and lemons' rendering, and he wondered whether the whole neigh-bourhood had reverted to second childhood. The door was opened immediately, but only by an inch or two, chained as it was to the lock.

'Yes?' the woman asked.

She looked wide awake and Neil was glad he hadn't
roused her from her bed. He hadn't rehearsed what he
would say, and as the words came out of his mouth he
realised how blatantly he was incriminating himself.

'There's a woman dead next door,' he said. 'I saw her
through the letter box. Murdered. There's blood. I've got
to use your phone.'

The woman's eyes widened in horror, and she gave a
little scream. Then a louder one, and she slammed the door
in his face. So hard, that it set off 'Oranges and lemons'
once again, proving a faulty connection. He waited until
the bells of St Clement's had pealed their last and he put
his ear to the door. The telephone must have been in the
hallway, for he heard the woman loud and clear.

'He said someone's been murdered.' Then a pause. 'Tall,'
the woman said. 'Nondescript really.'

Neil was offended. And fearful too. He had to report the
murder personally to put himself in the clear. He rushed
around the square and found a telephone box on the corner.
The police answered immediately, and he gave them the
same unrehearsed story he had spouted on the neighbour's
doorstep. When asked for his name, he gave it gladly and
then offered to stay at the address until they arrived. He
put down the phone with a certain relief, and with little
thought, though with a certain trepidation, he dialled again.
This time his father's number. It had been almost five years
since they had spoken. The very last time, he had put the
phone down on his father in mid-sentence. But sentence
enough to express his parental disappointment with his son.
He wondered whether his father had pickled the remains
of that sentence over the years and would now spill them
out, hearing how ragged the words were, how hurtful, and

above all, how pointless. He listened to his father's 'Hello?', and in its tone he heard the years that had passed. And his tongue froze in overwhelming regret. He simply couldn't respond. He knew he was not ready. But he had made a start, and that cheered him a little. In time he would talk to him, visit him even. He put the phone down. It was a start, he kept telling himself.

He heard the sirens and he knew he had to return to the scene of the crime and to assume a mournful air, as befitted the occasion. No one need know how inside his heart half leapt with joy.

A crowd had already gathered at the end of the street, pyjama-clad for the most part.

'There he is,' a voice shouted as he made his way through the crowd. 'That's him.' The woman who had slammed her door in his face was enjoying her fifteen minutes of fame.

Neil felt the accusing stares around him. He might as well be in the dock. He made his way to the policeman who stood at Miss Mayling's door, and announced himself as the telephone caller and the discoverer of the body.

'They'll need you to make a statement,' the policeman said. 'I'll get the Inspector.'

Neil waited, turning to return the crowd's stare. He had nothing to hide and he wanted them to be aware of it. Shortly after, the Inspector arrived and they were seen to have words together. Neil's address was taken and when all was written down, the Inspector shook his hand. 'Thank you, Mr Clarkson,' he said. 'We may need to be in touch.'

Neil made his way through the crowd, his father's 'Hello' echoing in his heart.

Miss Angela Mayling was childless, unmarried and lived alone. No known relatives. When Neil Clarkson read these details in the evening paper, he was not surprised. She was lonely and unhappy, and no doubt in the course of her interminable therapy, she had transferred her own lack of self-esteem to her patients. They were as much her crutch as she was theirs. It occurred to him that perhaps all shrinks worked in this way and that all of them needed a shrink of their own. A pure one, one untrammelled with personal baggage. But where was such a one to be found? Impossible, he decided. The entire profession was a swindle. And not only a swindle, it was close to a crime. Then he nurtured his delight in Miss Mayling's departure but he could not entirely erase a trace of regret that she was no more.

He went to her funeral, of course, and was saddened by the poor turn-out. Most of the congregation were police officers hoping for clues. They had expected perhaps that her patients would attend – they'd scoured her list and interviewed them all – but no patient would publicly declare himself as one who needed to be seen to. There was a modicum of shame attached to that need. Neil had already been 'outed' as the patient who had discovered the body, so he had no qualms about his presence at her funeral. He had had little respect for her, but the little that he had he would pay, and as her coffin sailed into the fire he felt an unmanufactured tear on his cheek.

He followed the progress of the police investigations in the papers. There had been house-to-house inquiries, but no witness had come forward. Miss Mayling lived in an area favoured by the retired who were wont to lie abed, and at seven-thirty in the morning, the time the coroner hazarded she had met her death, the milk bottles still sat on the doorsteps and the papers and post still jutted from the letter boxes. The paperboy and the milkman had made their calls at six-thirty, while Miss Mayling was still in the land of the living. Her regular patients all had confirmed alibis at the time, and the police drew a blank. Eventually, the murder of poor Miss Mayling slipped off the front pages and eventually did not merit even a back page reference. Neil Clarkson too lost interest and noted, with some delight, how much money he managed to put by. His father's 'Hello' still interrupted his dreams, and in the small hours he stifled a longing to hold Miss Mayling's helping hand.

On hearing of Miss Mayling's passing, DI Wilkins, like Neil Clarkson, was hopeful. He had immediately travelled to Birmingham, convinced now that he was dealing with a serial killer. The pattern was the same. Psychotherapist; untraceable patient; garrotting with a guitar string. None of these factors was easy to investigate. Especially the last. There were thousands of guitar players all over the country and even a non-guitar player could have access to strings. He wished the murder weapon could have been a string from a zither, a viola da gamba or even a harp. That would have narrowed the field a little. So he could not count on the guitar string as a reliable clue. Neither could he rely on finger- or fibre-prints. There simply weren't any. Neither was there any sign of forced entry. Poor Miss Mayling, like the previous victim, had invited her assailant into her own home. The similarities were hard to ignore but his serial-killer theory was only a hunch. He had nothing to substantiate it. And even less when, a week or so later, a prostitute in Soho was found murdered in a similar manner, a guitar string looped around her neck. But that could have been a copy-cat murder, Wilkins thought. He would not so easily abandon his serial theory. But he left Birmingham with little evidence that supported his opinion. The usual call for witnesses went out, but with no reliable response, and Wilkins' dreams were orchestrated with chords from a plaintive guitar.

Me again. *Ver-ine.* I went straight to the glass partition and waited for him. I put my hand on the glass,
spreading my fingers. I wanted him to see it as a sign of
welcome, one that he could match with his own. He smiled
as he sat in front of me, and I knew his first words.

'I am innocent. You know that, don't you?'

I nodded my head even before he had finished. It would
be his eternal prologue, and I wondered if my nodding
could last as long.

'How are they treating you?' I said into the machine.

He placed his hand to match my own. 'I miss you,' he
said.

I could have done without that so early on in the visit.
If he had to say it, he might have saved it till last when our
time was up and I would only have had to say, 'Me too,'
and leg it out of there. I smiled. He could make of that
what he would.

'Are they treating you well?' I asked again.

'I can't complain,' he said. 'I worry about getting used
to it here. And I mustn't do that because I'm not going
to be here much longer. I'm innocent. You believe that,
don't you.'

I nodded again and I thought that if I visited any more
often, my head would drop off. I'd never heard him so
talkative. He was ever a man of few words. Perhaps he spent
most of his time in silence, and he was using my visit to
practise his unrehearsed voice. I didn't know how to
respond. Innocent or guilty, he had no chance of getting

34

out of there. He hoped for a retrial but without fresh evidence, there was no chance of being heard a second time. And as far as everyone was concerned, it was all over and done with, and his fate was sealed.

I had decided to talk to him about the past, to reminisce about the happy times we had spent together. I had to find some subject of conversation. If it weren't for the telephones, I could have just looked at him and possibly held his hand. But you can't stare on the telephone, much less touch.

'I was thinking of the summer holidays we spent when the boys were little,' I started.

'I'm innocent. You know that,' he said.

He was clearly not interested in recalling the past and his constant plea of innocence was beginning to get on my nerves.

'You remember Margate sands?' I persisted. 'You used to make wonderful castles for the boys. All kinds, with moats and turrets. Even a drawbridge. You were so clever with your hands, Donald.'

The sound of his name surprised me. I had not used it for a long time. Not even to myself. It sounded like the name of a stranger.

'You were really clever,' I said again. I hoped to raise his spirits by praising him, and indeed he smiled as if it pleased him. I was encouraged.

'Why did we keep going back to Margate?' I asked him. 'We could have gone somewhere else for a change.'

'Margate was nice,' he said. 'It suited us. Besides the boys liked it.'

I was glad that he was prepared to make conversation.

'I always fancied somewhere in Devon,' I said. 'You used to go there a lot.'

I had mentioned Devon quite off the cuff, and I was not prepared for his reaction. Sudden tears rolled down his cheeks. What was Devon to him, or he to Devon, that he should weep for her? 'What's the matter, Donald?' I said, using the name again to make him less of a stranger.

'Nothing,' he said quickly. 'I don't want to talk about it.' That made two subjects he wouldn't talk about, I thought. Devon, and his lonely childhood. I made a note of them both for they merited further investigation. I went back to Margate, which was safer.

'That pension we stayed in,' I ploughed on. 'Mrs Price was her name, and she served a wonderful breakfast. D'you remember?'

He nodded.

I decided to itemise the menu. It was something to talk about. But in truth, I was bored with Margate. I was too disturbed by the brace of unmentionables he kept unspoken.

'Eggs, bacon, mushrooms, tomatoes, sausages, fried bread, fried potatoes. The whole lot. We got our money's worth there, Donald,' I said.

He nodded again. The man didn't need a telephone. I could just about cope with his nodding and smiling.

Then, suddenly, he began to drum his fingers on the glass, one after the other, as if he were practising the piano. And automatically, I drummed with him, finger after finger. Sometimes he varied the sequence and I followed. Or tried to. It became a game between us, and when I failed to keep up with him, he laughed and slapped the glass in victory. I was glad that we had found something wordless to do, and when the warder interrupted our game he showed some annoyance.

'One to me,' he said into the phone. 'I'll keep the score.'

He smiled again, and as he was led away he threw me a kiss, which I returned through the glass. Though with little reason, he looked happy. I think that at last he had something to look forward to. And I would let him win. Every time.

THE DIARY

THREE DOWN. SIX TO GO.

I am cross. Someone has tried to steal my thunder. A guitar string is *my* signature. No one else's. Anyway, they caught him. He was tried and found guilty. He's serving life. And serves him right. You don't murder someone just for the kicks of it. You've got to have a pretty good reason. Good motivation. You have to be on a mission. Like me.

It's been some time since my last sortie. Harry Winston and Angela Mayling are still on the back-burner and it looks as if they might stay there for a while. As usual, there were no witnesses and no fingerprints. As usual, patients have been questioned, in confidence, of course, but none of them seemed to have motive enough for murder. Was I lucky, I wondered. Or just very clever? Secretly, I believe that God is on my side. He knows that my mission is just.

I was ready for my next strike, and I wanted variation. I decided to alter my disguise radically. I would dress as a woman. It wouldn't be the first time, but I'd never risked it abroad. It would be fun. And if I was witnessed, old Wilkins would have fresh fish to fry. I have access to frocks. Verry's. She knows about this little hobby of mine and she gladly gives me free access to her wardrobe. Sometimes of an evening we sit together and dine or watch television, and I flounce my petticoats around her and we have a good laugh. She's a real brick, my Verry. Never questions anything. Just goes along with it. Take Devon, for instance. That's where I keep my fantasy client. But she really believes in him; asks me to bring her back some clotted cream. And I do. You can get it

38

anywhere in London. I wouldn't want to disappoint her. Verry's just right for me.

To further vary my sorties, and to keep Wilkins on the hop, I chose to go to Wales. Barry Island, a seaside resort, not far from Cardiff. I could drive there and back in a day. My target was a Miss Bronwen Hughes. I knew she lived alone, because I'd read a profile about her in a professional journal. She was well thought of, apparently. On the down-side, she claimed that she had never made a professional mistake. So that, even when called for, she would never apolo-gise. Well, Miss Hughes, I thought, I'll give you something to be sorry for.

I took a carrier-bag of Verry's clothes and make-up, and I changed in my office. I left London very early, and happily reached the M4 by six o'clock. My appointment was for nine-thirty. I enjoyed that ride. Petticoats donate a certain freedom and often I fingered my flouncy skirt, and I was tempted more than once to get out of the car and twirl on the lay-by. But that would have to wait for my return journey when I could risk a service station, and mince my way around the self-service and eat like a lady.

I reached Barry Island just before nine o'clock. I parked my car by the sea, and strode down to the shoreline. I was tempted to take a paddle, to hook my skirt into my knickers and primp my hair, an inconspicuous brown wig. But it was too cold for a paddle and moreover I had omitted to shave my legs. Even in my disguise which, take it from me, could have fooled anybody, it would have been folly to take such a risk. So I idled around for a while then promptly turned up at Miss Hughes' little cottage. I put on my gloves and rang the bell.

She answered the door herself. I could have done her there and then, in the hallway, as I had so briefly dispatched Miss

Mayling, but I was feeling rather frisky. It must have been the sea air. I thought I'd let her have a small go at me.

She led me into her parlour and motioned me into a chair. Then she sat herself at her desk.

'I have a note here,' she said, 'that I am expecting a Mr Henry Willes. That presumably is your name?'

So I hadn't fooled her, after all. And I was none too pleased.

'Well that's my problem, you see,' I said. 'That's why I need help. I'm obsessed, you see, with cross-dressing, and I'd like to . . . well . . . be cured.'

She stared at me with little sympathy.

'Tell me about yourself,' she said.

'Like what?' I asked.

'When you were a child. What was that like?'

I started out on a fictitious childhood. I invented an abusive father and an alcoholic mother. I even threw in a grannie who was senile. I went on and on about my miserable childhood, and I wondered why she didn't interrupt or say something. I suppose she wanted me to spill it all out, and then she might deign to offer a word of wisdom. But I wasn't going to wait for that. Miss Hughes, however well thought of, was beginning to get on my nerves. It would be a pleasure to kill her.

But suddenly she actually spoke, looking at me with a certain interest and I thought I might as well grant her her say. She sorted through some papers on her desk and then passed one of them into my gloved hand. On it was a drawing, a sketch in black ink that stretched across the page and, to my eye, represented nothing.

'What is that a picture of, do you think?'

'Looks like a dragon,' I said. 'A bit like my grannie.'

It didn't look like anything at all, but I thought that my

interpretation would please her. And indeed it did, for she smiled. 'Good,' she said. 'Now look at this one.'

Another drawing was delivered, this time patches of doodling spread across the page. Again I called on my fictitious grannie, and I said that it reminded me of Grannie's knitting.

Miss Hughes smiled again. She had cottoned on to Grannie as a key figure.

'Did she tell you stories when you were a child?' she asked.

'She told me the story of Little Red Ridinghood,' I said. 'I liked that one, and she told it often. I especially liked the part when the fox dressed up as the grannie. I used to laugh at that.' I couldn't have given Miss Hughes a clearer clue. But I was fed up with Grannie and I needed to be on my way. So I rose and took the string out of my bodice pocket. When she saw my weapon, she paled. She realised exactly what I was up to, and she attempted to flee, but after a few steps she froze in terror. I sat her down, and I went behind her and did the usual business. I was getting pretty good at it by now. I waited for her to snuff and I apologised to Wilkins for leading him such a merry dance. I left the house, uncaring whether or not I was seen, for no one would suspect a woman of such a crime. I twirled my skirt before getting into the car. On my way home, I ate lunch at a service station, and leaving the M4 I made a detour to a shop in Pimlico which sold clotted cream from Devon.

THREE DOWN. SIX TO GO.

It took five patients to turn away from an unanswered
bell, before the police were alerted. A neighbour had
noticed the slow comings and quicker goings of the callers.
PC Gower of the local force came to investigate and immediately put two and two together. Or rather, one and one.
The psychotherapist and the guitar string. He was delighted
and he was going to keep it to himself. He knew about the
killings – all police authorities had been alerted, and he had
heard about Detective Inspector Wilkins' frustration. But
bugger the DI, he thought. He was going to handle this
one himself.

He reported his findings to the station. He would need
their back-up. They all agreed that little Barry Island should
go it alone. It would put the place on the map and be good
for tourism. Though it would have to offer a lot more than
a notorious murder to attract visitors. Barry Island was not
exactly Palm Beach in Florida. But they couldn't keep it
out of the local papers, and shortly the news spread to
Wilkins' ear. And off he went down the M4 to investigate.

He had the grace to praise PC Gowers' deductions and
the constable had to be satisfied with that small acknowledgement. Together they visited the scene of the crime,
and found what Wilkins expected to find. No sign of a
break-in. Not a single fingerprint. And on questioning and
house to house, not a single witness. Just a guitar string
around a garrotted neck.

'We have a serial killer on our hands,' Wilkins announced
on his return to London. Three murders following a similar

pattern was enough to merit the term 'serial'. It was time
to call in the forensic psychologist.

Dr Arbuthnot was occasionally ashamed of himself, for
he rarely got it right. In the case of a serial killer of old
ladies, he had hazarded a man of brute strength who hated
his mother. The confessing killer turned out to be a slender
young woman who was an orphan. In another case of serial
rape, he had diagnosed a middle-aged man of athletic build,
who turned out to be a priapic seventeen-year-old boy.
Occasionally he got it right, but only by making deductions that anyone of reasonable intelligence could have made
without the benefit of medical training. To be fair to Dr
Arbuthnot, in the case of the shrink killer he had little to
work on. But he had a go, and came out with the declaration that the murderer was probably a psychotherapist
himself, one who had been struck off the register. He had
no connection to offer with regard to the guitar string or
the irregular intervals between the attacks. He acknowledged that this was a significant factor but until and unless
it repeated itself, he could draw no conclusions.

Wilkins then organised an investigation into all unfrocked
psychotherapists. But there were precious few.
Incompetence and criminal negligence in such a profession
is very hard to prove. Witnesses tend to be patients, and
their very need for therapy in the first place does not recom-
mend their reliability.

Wilkins didn't know where to turn. Inwardly he prayed
for another killing, and even another, until a careless clue
was left behind. He avoided the Chief Superintendent at
the station and he dreaded the moment when he would be
called into his office to give account. Once he bumped into
him in the corridor, and he faltered in his steps.

'Press on, Wilkins,' the Chief said, as he passed him. 'Press on,' and he flashed him a smile.

The encounter afforded a margin of relief, but Wilkins had no idea how he could press on, and in what direction. In all three cases he had exhausted his inquiries. Most of the patients had willingly come forward, if only to express their indifference. But none had been actively hostile, hostile enough to commit murder. Until this time, the killer had chosen therapists who were on the professional register and Wilkins dreaded that he might well spread his net wider and include unauthorised healers, who were legion. He'd been deeply disappointed with Dr Arbuthnot's report and he himself began to have doubts about the whole profession. His sister suffered from depression and she'd been in and out of therapists' consulting rooms and on and off the couches of sundry psychiatrists for years, and much good had it done her – until her GP prescribed simple anti-depressant pills and she now functioned fully like a normal person. Somebody out there had a grudge, Wilkins concluded, a bitter hatred against the whole profession. But where could he turn? How could he press on? He simply had to wait for the next assault.

I slept very badly again last night and felt unwell when I woke up. I didn't think I could manage the journey to the prison. Donald would be disappointed, but I just didn't feel up to it. I phoned the authorities to let them know why I wouldn't be visiting, and also to tell Donald that it was only a cold and that I would be up and about in no time.

So I had a whole day in which to do nothing and I thought I'd pamper myself a bit. Stay in bed, look at television. Eat chocolate. So there was I, lying in bed, watching the breakfast show when my doorbell rang. Now I hardly get any visitors, especially since the trial. The journalists don't come any more. I'm yesterday's news. I wondered who it could be and the thought crossed my mind not to answer the door. But whoever it was rang again. And again. I got out of bed, and through the stained glass of the front door, I made out the shape of a woman. Confirmed by a feathered hat. I drew my dressing-gown around me, and without undoing the chain – I have to be extra careful nowadays – I opened the door a few inches, wide enough to find out what the caller wanted.

She was a good-looking woman, about my age – perhaps a little older. She smiled at me, a nervous smile, and I sensed she wanted a favour, though I could not imagine what good I could do for anybody. But I found myself willing to try. I was lonely and I welcomed company, whoever she was. But I didn't unchain the door.

'Can I help you?' I asked.

'It's a delicate matter, Mrs Dorricks,' she said. 'Can I come in?'

'You're not from the newspapers, are you?' I asked.

'No,' she said. 'It's a personal matter.'

I believed her, and I took the chain off the door.

'Come in,' I said, and led her into the kitchen. I had already decided to make her a cup of tea. Her voice was gentle and she seemed very friendly. I told her to sit down and I put the kettle on.

'It's a lovely day today,' I said. I wanted to postpone learning the reason for her visit. I sensed it would be disturbing, and a cup of tea between us would make it more palatable. I set out the cups and put some biscuits on a plate.

'That's very kind of you,' she said. 'A cup of tea would be most refreshing.

I looked at her properly for the first time, and there was something familiar about her face. I knew I had seen it before, and often, but I couldn't remember where. I kept it in my mind's eye as I filled the teapot, and in a flash I saw her at Donald's trial, sitting on the same bench, day after day. Not far from my own reserved place. Her visit clearly had to do with Donald and my curiosity was slightly piqued. I poured the tea for us both and offered her a biscuit. Then I settled myself down so that I faced her squarely, ready for anything she had to say. But nothing on earth could have prepared me for her introduction.

'My name's Emma,' she said.

I envied her her confidence. With a name like Emma, so phonetic, so unvariable, self-confidence is assured.

'I'm pleased to meet you, Emma,' I said. I refrained from announcing myself.

'Don't you know of me?' the woman asked.

'I saw you at the trial,' I said. 'But I don't know you. Should I?'

'I'm Emma,' she said again. 'Emma Dorricks.'

I was confused. I knew practically nothing about Donald's family. He might have had an aunt somewhere. Or cousins. I was heartened. There might be someone else to share my burden.

'Dorricks,' I said. 'Then we must be related.'

'Not really,' she said. 'Don't you know about me?' she asked again.

I shook my head, further confused.

'Just like Donald,' she said. 'Kept his mouth shut on everything.'

I agreed with her, but still could not guess at her part in it.

'I'm Emma Dorricks,' she said again. 'Donald's first wife.'

I put down the biscuit I was holding in my hand. If I'd bitten on it, it would have choked me. But I took a gulp of tea to swallow the lump in my throat. A lump of astonishment rather than sorrow. I recalled our wedding day in the register office. There had been papers to sign and perhaps one of them may have noted a divorce. But I didn't read them. I was too excited at the thought of my future. Then the thought occurred to me that perhaps Donald was a bigamist.

'Were you divorced?' My voice was wavering.

'Oh yes,' Emma said. 'You're absolutely legal.'

'Any children?' I asked. Another matter that I had to settle. I prayed that their union had been childless. I wanted something from Donald that nobody else had had.

'No,' she said. 'Fortunately. Otherwise I would never have left him.'

'You left him?' I asked. How could any woman leave such a loving man? 'But why?'

'My fault. My fault entirely. And I regret it. But he was so clammed up all the time. We were together for two years, and in all that time he never talked about himself. Refused to answer questions. Told me there was nothing that I needed to know. I couldn't stand it. I started to go out on my own. I met another man. One who never stopped talking. Within six months I knew all I wanted to know about him, and a lot more that I didn't. I wished he'd shut up. I missed Donald's silences and I longed for peace. But by then it was too late. He'd met you, he told me, and he wanted a divorce. I envied you then, I have to confess. He's a good man is Donald. I can't believe he's guilty. Not Donald. He doesn't have it in him.'

I warmed to the woman. She could easily become a friend and I looked forward to a sharing of our discontent.

'Why have you come?' I asked.

'I want a favour,' she said. 'I'd like to visit him. I still love him, you know, in my own way. I watched him every day at the trial. I was full of regrets. I think he can't have many visitors and he must be terribly lonely. But I need a permit to visit him so he has to be willing to see me. And I'm not too sure about that. So I've come to ask you to persuade him. To tell him about my visit. And all my regrets.'

I pictured Emma's hand on the glass partition and for a moment, I resented her print over mine. 'But I'm not supposed to know anything about you,' I said.

'But now you do. Please, please, I beg you. Just ask him to see me.'

'But why do you want to see him so much? And after all this time?'

'I never told him I was sorry,' Emma said. 'And I pity him.'

'You mustn't pity him,' I said. 'Pity is difficult to live with. I ought to know. I avoid it if I can.'

Emma had begun to cry. I poured her some more tea, trying not to pity her.

'I'll talk to Donald,' I said. It was still early and I could still visit him. I could ring the prison and tell them I was coming after all.

Emma rose from the table. 'Here's my address and tele-phone number.' She drew a piece of paper out of her bag. She had already prepared it. 'Please, I beg you, be in touch with me. Even if you can't persuade him,' she said, 'I'd like us to stay in touch.'

She was smiling at me, and I sensed she was as lonely as I was, but unlike me, her loneliness was aggravated by regret. I was glad I had little to be sorry for. I had been a good wife to Donald but only because he'd been a good husband to me. I told her I'd be in touch. I was anxious for her to leave. I had to prepare for my visit. She under-stood, straightened her hat and picked up her bag.

'I wish you a good visit,' she said.

As soon as she'd gone, I phoned the prison. I told them I felt much better and that I would be taking up my visiting permit.

I took special care with my dressing. I wanted to look my best for Donald. I was careful with my make-up. He used to love watching me as I applied the rouge and mascara. And especially when I painted my nails. I think the smell of the polish turned him on. Then my best linen suit and barely black stockings. He loved that colour. I looked in the mirror and introduced myself as the second Mrs

Dorricks. It was a title I had to get used to. On the train, I tried not to rehearse what I would say to him. I tried not to imagine how he would react to the news of my visitor. I concentrated on remembering our past together, a time when Emma Dorricks was unknown to me, a time when I had no predecessor, when I was his first much-loved discovery. By the time I reached the prison gates, Emma Dorricks had been forgotten and I had to remind myself why I had changed my mind to come and visit him.

I placed myself in front of the glass partition and put my hand on my regular spot though I didn't think that Donald would feel like playing after he'd heard about my discovery. I expected anger. Even denial. But I would weather them both, since both would be pointless. I decided that I wouldn't spring the news on him straight away. I would wait until visiting time was nearing its end. Until then, he could tell me how innocent he was and I would do my nodding bit, and we'd still have time to play our game.

He was smiling as he entered, and immediately put his hand to match mine and together we picked up the phones. 'You shouldn't have come,' he said, 'if you weren't feeling well. I was worried about you. You have to take care of yourself, sweetheart.'

I felt that all the wind had been taken out of my sails. My Donald was a man of few words, who had seldom given voice to his feelings. The word 'sweetheart' was as foreign to his mouth as it was to my ear. Even so, it had rolled so easily off his tongue, it shattered my hearing. I suddenly loved him so much for his caring. I didn't want to think that I had shared that caring with anybody else. But most of all, I didn't want *him* to think so. I would not mention the name of Emma. That name was his history. Not mine.

That Emma event, like most others in his life, had been kept from me, perhaps because of his caring and for my own protection. I would not be Emma's message carrier. In my own recording of events, she had never happened.

Donald seemed in a good mood. Happy almost, although I couldn't imagine why. We played our fingers game for a while, and he won each time. His skill was greater than mine.

'Have you seen the boys?' he asked.

I noticed that his smile was fading. 'No,' I said. 'They are not in touch with me.' I wanted to share my regret with him, to assure him that I, too, was part of that same deprivation.

'Pity,' he said. 'It would do me good to see them. Even though they think I don't deserve a visit.'

I said nothing. His fingers were inert on the glass. He had lost his appetite for the game and I decided that, on my return, I would do my best to contact our boys and to persuade them to visit him.

'Cheer up,' I said to him. 'How do you spend your time?' I had never asked him such a question. I didn't want to hint at his permanence in the place.

'In the workshop,' he said. 'But I'm beginning to paint. I'm learning. A teacher comes twice a week.'

This news heartened me, as would any event that enabled him to take his mind off his incarceration.

'Can I see one of your paintings?' I asked.

'Next time,' he said. 'I've not finished the one I'm working on.'

Then I began to doubt whether he had even started it, and was just trying to cheer me up. 'I look forward to it,' I said. I tried to start the finger game again, but he would not cooperate. It's not a game for one, any more than tennis, and my fluttering fingers looked silly on the glass. I took my hand away, and he did the same. I was glad when the warder came and gently touched Donald's shoulder.

'Now, you look after yourself,' were Donald's last words into the phone. I assured him that I would. I also added that I loved him. He reclipped his phone and pressed his lips on the pane. And I matched his with my own. As he was leaving he turned and pursed his lips once more.

'Emma came to see me,' I whispered, because I knew he could not hear me. But I had promised Emma that I would try.

On the train back to London, I wondered how I could persuade my boys to visit their father. That would be the first step towards a reconciliation with Donald. Even if they considered him guilty, I would remind them of their boyhood and of the gentle role that Donald had played during those years. They could visit him just for that, for having been a good and caring father. Whatever they now thought, they had a duty to acknowledge those years. I felt myself growing angry and resenting them. Hating them even. It simply wasn't fair that I had to bear the burden of his innocence alone.

THE DIARY

FOUR DOWN. FIVE TO GO.

I had to laugh when I read the police psychologist's report.
It was in all the papers. Though it didn't surprise me – I
would not have expected any trace of imagination from that
quarter. The poor sod reckons I am an unfrocked shrink. As
if anybody in their right mind would have opted for such a
profession in the first place. And I mean, precisely, in their
right mind. For a truly right mind has no need to foist its
own hang-ups on others in the name of healing. Old
Arbuthnot also pointed out that the irregular intervals
between the murders might be a significant factor. Well, I
have foxed him and my most recent attack was nine months
after my last. Let's see what Arbuthnot makes of that one.
He'll probably deduce some gestation theory and phrase it in
psychobabble. He has at least saved us from his theories
regarding the guitar string. He'll never get to the bottom of
that one, I promise you. So witter on, Dr Arbuthnot, and
may you choke on your own gobbledegook.

I began to feel a little sorry for old Wilkins and his foot-
sore slog around the country in pursuit. So out of the kindness of my heart, I decided to stick to London for my next
sortie, so that both he and I wouldn't have too far to go.

I had to attend the school sports day. My boys were in the
races and I had promised them to enter for the hundred yards
fathers' sprint. I was glad of the diversion. I welcomed any
physical exercise. I needed to keep fit for my mission. Martin
won the long jump and Matthew broke all records with his
discus throw. Verry was delighted, and I was proud of them

both. And nervous too, because my own event was coming up. I wanted them to be as proud of me. I lined up among the other fathers. The competition would be keen, for all of them looked very fit. There were about ten of us and I was determined to be first. I wouldn't be satisfied with any other placing. It was this determination, I think, that injected my heels and I ran like a hare to the finishing post, leaving them all behind. I heard Verry and the boys' cheers above all the others. I had won, not for myself, but for them. I saw my victory as a good omen for my next strike. That night, Verry cooked us a special supper, but my exertions had tired me and I went early to bed.

I had made an evening appointment with one Alistair Morris. My first night attack. I was excited. I had checked on Morris and found out that he was a bachelor who lived alone in north London. Not too far away, either for myself or for Wilkins. I discovered, too, that Morris was a Jungian therapist. I was not too sure what that meant but I was curious as to his methods.

Once again, I dressed as a woman, though this time in a skirted suit and high heels. I varied the wig too. I fancied myself as a blonde. I had made the appointment in the name of Priscilla Downes. I liked the ring of it, and I practised the name as I drove towards my quarry. As was my wont, I parked my car a little distance from my target's home. There were few people around. But I wasn't worried; I was in drag and, in any case, it was already dark. But I made sure that Morris's street was empty before I rang his bell, and that no net curtains had been raised. I hesitated before ringing. I was feeling too cocky, too sure of myself. I was still relishing the aftertaste of my fathers-race victory. Yet I couldn't hesitate too long. I primped my wig, and rang his bell. When asked, I announced myself through the intercom.

'Miss Downes.' I offered my contralto, the highest I could risk and I waltzed inside. I noticed a suitcase in the hall, suggesting arrival or departure. But, either way, it wasn't going anywhere. My womanly gait gave me confidence, which was boosted by the sight of my target. He was of slight build, thin, bony almost, and considerably shorter than I. What pleased me most was his neck: scraggy and of small diameter. He could be quickly and cleanly dispatched.

'Miss Downes,' he stated. 'Please sit down.' And almost in the same breath, 'Of course, you are not Miss Downes. *Mr* Downes rather.'

All my self-assurance evaporated. This was the second time I'd been rumbled, and I could happily have killed the man there and then.

'Well, that's what I've come about.' I relaxed into my baritone voice and recited my rehearsed lines.

'Shall we try a little something?' he said.

He was not asking my permission, for he didn't wait for an answer. 'I'm going to give you a word, and I want you to say, without thinking about it – that's important – I want you to give me a word that comes into your mind. Shall we try it?'

Again it was not a request for permission. This must be the Jungian method, I thought. Free association, I think they call it. I decided to let him play with me for a while.

'Are you ready?' he asked.

I nodded.

'Mother,' he said.

'Father,' I hit back at him.

'Dark?'

'Moon' was my response.

'Dream?'

'Wake.'

'Business?'

'Money.'

Thus we ping-ponged with as yet no point scored.

'Sport?' he tried again.

'Skipping.'

Then he served an ace that I couldn't return.

'Rope,' he yelled.

I felt assaulted, invaded, and I was certainly not going to play any more. How dare he throw me a word that not even *I* could pronounce, one that I could barely imagine. He had sailed too close to the wind. He had chanced his arm and although he was not aware of it, he was nudging my crusade off course. He had to be shoved out of the way.

I got up quickly.

'I'm going to kill you,' I said. 'I have to. I'm on a mission.'

And it was that word, that mention of my inflexible crusade, it was that word that spelt out my cause as just. I moved towards the desk. I took out my string and dangled it in front of him. Then he realised what I was about and he rose, trembling with fear and rage. He threw himself on me and tried to pin me to the ground. But I was stronger and I threw him off. His resistance excited me, and knowing my superior strength I was content to spar a little. Then he kicked me in the groin and took the wind out of me. My anger was greater than my pain, and I shoved him back into his seat, laced his scraggy neck, and did the business. I avoided the blood as I tested his pulse. I was wearing one of Verry's favourite suits and I didn't want it stained.

I left the house quickly. There were some people about, but by now it was very dark and I doubt if any of them saw me leaving. However, to be on the safe side, I did not return to my car. I decided I would walk towards the Underground station, and then lose myself in its passages. In any case, I needed to walk. I needed to clear my head. Usually after a killing, I felt elated and I would sing on my way home. But this time there was no feeling of triumph. On the contrary, I felt deeply depressed. It was Mr Morris's resistance that had unnerved me. He had no right to put up a struggle. He had met his just end. To date, I had killed four people. In the terms of my mission, they were guilty, each one of them, and each one of them deserved to die. I must not question that assumption. Never. Else my crusade would be denied its purpose. Yet, after Morris, for the first time since I had set out on my mission, I itched with scruple.

I could not afford misgivings. I could not suffer qualms. I walked slowly back to my car. I went over in my mind all the reasons why my mission was imperative, and why I had started on it in the first place. The whole 'why' of it. So I analysed it, imaged it, picture after compelling picture, and by the time I reached my car I felt appeased and I hummed my way home.

FOUR DOWN. FIVE TO GO.

When Wilkins was informed of the Morris murder, he was delighted. This time, he was positive the killer had slipped up. He must have. He was optimistic, even though the odds were stacked against him. For it was a good three weeks before Mr Morris's body was discovered. Information from a neighbour revealed that Mr Morris had booked a three-week holiday in Ibiza and the local newsagent confirmed that his paper delivery had been stopped. Other neighbours, when questioned, agreed that Mr Morris was a 'queer bloke', a phrase used by many of them, some with a curled lip and others with a sly smile. Such information did not hearten Wilkins, for it pointed to a very specific motive for the killing. A rejected lover, perhaps. He had known of similar cases. The killer could well have been some other than the man he was after. Nevertheless, he lived in hope of a clue.

It was a suspicious postman who had alerted the police. He had noticed that much post had accumulated and the box was full. He had opened the flap to push the letters through, and had reeled from the abominable smell. He'd invited a neighbour to share the aroma, and both suspected its source.

'It was bound to happen one day,' the neighbour said, and the postman didn't know what she was talking about.

Wilkins almost sprinted to the north London suburb, photographer and police pathologist panting at his heels. By the time they arrived, the neighbours had gathered outside on Mr Morris's neat front lawn. Wilkins ordered them back to their houses and saw to it as his aide gently prised open the front door and staggered backwards, choked by the smell. The investigators muffled their mouths with scarves or handkerchiefs and entered.

They did not have to look for the body. The smell led them to the spot. Enough was left of poor Mr Morris to reveal the method of his murder – a neat guitar string around the neck; and, after meticulous examination, not a single print of any kind in sight, nor any sign of a break-in. It could have been a copy-cat killing, Wilkins thought. It could well have been a rejected lover, one who had been invited inside, or perhaps even used his own key, who had wreaked his vengeance. The pathologist knelt over the body. He could not be precise as to the day and time of the killing. The rate of decomposition indicated that Morris had been dead for at least three to four weeks. At that stage he could not be more specific. The muffled photographer went about his business, and to an audience of muttering net curtains what was left of poor Mr Morris's body was parcelled away in an unmarked van. Wilkins returned to his desk and, although he knew it was wicked, prayed for another killing.

No address book had been found at Mr Morris's house. And no diary. Just a filing cabinet containing details of his patients. Wilkins underwent the dreary task of interviewing them all. Except one, a Mr Johnson, who was never at home. But Wilkins attached little importance to his absence. Throughout his long investigations he had found that patients in general had little to offer by way of clues and their attitude to each killing varied between delight and sorrow. Mr Johnson might well be on holiday, and perhaps unaware of his counsellor's demise. As he sat at his desk, mulling over the evidence, or sheer lack of it, that he had collected during the course of his therapist inquiries, he was called by the front office. A Mr Jeremy Johnson wanted to see him on a matter of urgency. The name rang like wedding bells in Wilkins' ear.

'Has he stated his business?' Wilkins asked, though he knew the answer.

'The shrinks,' the messenger said.

Wilkins composed himself. He envisioned a confession. He felt it in his bones. But he must beware of a hoax. There were enough nutters around who, for reasons unknown, confessed to murder. But he did not think Johnson was one of them. He would be gentle with him. Very gentle. Until he was convinced by his confession. Then he would spit on him.

He told the messenger to bring the man to his office. He arranged a chair in front of his desk so that he could look him squarely in the face. Gentle, gentle, until he was taken to the interrogation room. Then perhaps he would be offered a cup of tea.

He stood up as his door opened. 'Come in, Mr Johnson,' he said. 'Sit down.'

He settled himself behind the desk and looked directly at his visitor. And what he saw did not please him. The man was wearing make-up, unashamed mascara on his eyes and rouge on his cheeks. He might well have been a rejected lover, who had killed for that reason, but no way could he be a serial killer. The man was perfumed too, and the smell wafted teasingly across the desk.

'What can I do for you?' Wilkins asked.

Mr Johnson came straight to the point. 'I've come to confess,' he said. He put his hands together in a cathedral shape, his long fingers trembling, and Wilkins noticed that his lacquered nails were slightly chipped.

'Confess to what?' he asked.

'I murdered Mr Morris,' he said.

'Would you say that again?' Wilkins asked, playing for time. He could not yet make up his mind whether the man was a hoaxer.

'Like I said,' Mr Johnson insisted, 'I murdered Mr Morris.'

'How did you murder him?' asked Wilkins. The 'whys' could come later.

'I garrotted him. With a guitar string.'

'Did you wear gloves?' Wilkins asked.

'Of course. I didn't want to leave fingerprints.'

'Did you get blood on your clothes?'

'No. I took care of that. I stood well away.'

'And how did you get into the house?'

'Mr Morris let me in. As he did, every Tuesday, Wednesday and Thursday at six o'clock. I was always his last patient of the day.'

'Patient?' Wilkins was slightly thrown.

'Of course. Why else do you think I went there?'

So he was not necessarily a rejected lover, at least not by Mr Morris, Wilkins thought. He had saved the crucial question till last. The 'how' of the murder, the guitar string and the garrotte, the unforced entry, the lack of clues, all these facts could have been garnered from newspaper reports. And they didn't prove Johnson as the killer. The reason for the murders had never been reported because it was not known by anybody. Not even himself. So he paused before asking the vital question.

'Tell me, Mr Johnson,' he said. 'Why did you kill him?

What terrible reason did you have for taking a good man's life?'

'He wasn't a good man,' Mr Johnson said. 'He let me down.'

'In which way?' Wilkins held on to his gentle tone, although it called for effort.

'He was going on holiday. Three whole weeks.' His voice trembled. 'What right did he have to leave me? What was I to do for three weeks without his help?'

'What have you done before when he went away?' Wilkins asked.

'But he never did, you see. He wasn't a man for holidays. The odd weekend, here and there. But never a weekday. Never. He knew I couldn't manage without him.'

'How long have you been his patient?' Wilkins asked.

'Nine years, come August,' Mr Johnson said with a certain pride.

Three times a week? For nine years? Time enough to be cured of whatever condition Mr Johnson suffered from, Wilkins thought, and it was not difficult to guess what that condition was. The rouge, mascara and nail varnish proclaimed it. 'That's a long time,' Wilkins said for lack of anything else to say. 'May I ask how much you paid for this treatment?'

'Thirty pounds,' Mr Johnson said.

'A week?'

'No. A session.'

'Ninety pounds a week then,' Wilkins said. He tried to tot it all up in his head but it was too complicated and unashamedly he wrote down the sum on a piece of paper, and like an old-fashioned schoolboy he did his multiplication. Five down, carry four, until he reached the obscene sum of four thousand six hundred and eighty pounds a year. And he continued on his paper to multiply it by nine.

'Forty-two thousand, one hundred and twenty pounds,' he said aloud and he wondered how, for all that money, Mr Morris had bettered his patient's condition. Perhaps the chipped nail varnish was a sign that Mr Johnson was losing interest in his little hobby but it still seemed an awful lot of money to pay out for a bottle of nail-varnish remover. Slowly Wilkins began to lose sympathy for the killer's victim. Even with one patient, he reckoned that lot earned twice as much as he did, and probably twenty times that much, according to their patient lists. He decided that the killer might well be motivated by envy and he would put this theory to Dr Arbuthnot, whose job it was to take it into account. Although he knew that poor Mr Johnson – he had transferred his sympathies from the victim to the man sitting in front of him – was a hoaxer, he nevertheless decided to keep him in custody for a while. He hoped that he would learn from him something about the therapist's profession, some facts that would enlighten him and perhaps give him clues to the killer proper.

As he ordered his detention, he told his officers not to get too excited. Johnson would probably turn out to be a false trail, he told them, but one who might uncover some useful clues. 'Treat him gently,' he told them. 'I'm pretty sure he's innocent.'

Wilkins was not too disappointed. Although his hopes had been shattered, he had found the interview useful. It had cast a new light on the case in hand. It had caused his own prejudices to shift, and he began to question his previous assumptions. He felt positive and confident. 'It may take time,' he said to himself, 'but I shall run this fox to earth.'

It's my birthday today. I'm forty-seven. My first birthday without Donald. He always arranged a birthday treat for me. We'd go out to dinner. Or the theatre. And he'd take great care to choose presents he knew I would like. I'm sad today. I'm sad because Donald's not here. But sad too about my boys. They haven't been in touch with me since Donald was taken. They don't want me to know where they are living though I'm sure they're together, and in London somewhere. They both work in the City. Insurance. And in the same company. When they left, they told me they were going to change their surname. Dorricks is not like Jones or Smith. It's a singular name, and they didn't want to be associated with it. So I don't even know what my boys are called. I wish they would get in touch. I want to persuade them to go and see their father. If only I could remember the name of their firm. Perhaps Donald knows. I'll ask him next time I visit.

I don't feel like getting up this morning. I want to sleep my birthday away. Birthdays are times when you think about your future. You daydream and you plan. But the future I have to look forward to is bleak and lonely, and when I'm in a low mood I find it easy to fall asleep. God is good sometimes.

I was tempted to go and see if there was any post before I went back to bed. I had no reason to expect birthday cards, but I couldn't help myself going to the letter box. And indeed, there was one letter, and in a pink envelope, so I knew that someone had remembered. I looked at the stamp and saw the franking of H. M. Prison, and I knew who it was from. I had half hoped that my boys would have remembered, but I had to make do with Donald. Which upset me a bit, for it was all because of him that the boys had not written. I get these moments of not liking Donald very much, yet sometimes I love him as deeply as I did in the very beginning. Between the loving and the hating, and the not knowing and not wanting to know, between my total belief in his innocence and my disturbing doubts, between all these things, I was mightily confused. I couldn't face the reality, because I was not quite sure what the reality was.

I opened Donald's card. Inside was a painting, a river with a weeping willow, signed Donald Dorricks. And I loved him once again. There was a river quite near where I used to live, with a willow on its banks. We used to go there often, Donald and I, when we were courting. He must be dwelling on those times, I thought, those happy times before people said he did terrible things. But they lied. Not my Donald. He's innocent. And I ought to know. I lived with him all those years. I would have noticed something, something not quite right. But everything seemed normal. He got depressed sometimes. But don't we all? Nothing abnormal about that. It's a good painting he's done for me, and I'm glad he has a flair for it, because it will help him pass his time. His life, really, because that's his sentence. He'll have to do at least fifteen years before he's eligible for parole. I'll be sixty-two then, and he'll be seventy-three – an old man. I was beginning to feel sad again, and I crawled back into bed and put his card under my pillow.

Someone was ringing the doorbell, and the sound woke me. I was not expecting anybody so I tried to go back to sleep. But the ringing was insistent. I looked at my watch. It was already twelve o'clock. I'd slept almost half my birthday away, and with luck I could get rid of my caller and sleep away the other half. I dragged on a dressing-gown and went to the door. Through the coloured glass pane, I could see two shadows. I watched them and saw the one merge with the other. Always together. Always one. My boys. I no longer wanted to sleep. That shadow was a reality I could face. I was trembling. It was almost a year since I had set eyes on them, and as I tried to compose myself they rang the bell again. I knew that they were anxious to be indoors, away from the net-curtain stares, those down-the-nose looks they had fled to avoid. So I opened the door quickly and they brushed past me avoiding a doorstep greeting. But once inside, safely housed in their father's ambivalent innocence, they embraced me, the two of them together, wishing me a happy birthday.

'We're taking you for lunch,' Matthew said. 'We've booked a table. Go and get dressed.'

I have to confess it was a relief to leave them for a while. What does one do with all those words, all that vocabulary chock-a-block in your mouth, utterances you cannot utter, hopes you cannot express and, above all, love so frayed by hurt?

As I dressed, I imagined their conversation downstairs. They were planning their strategy. How to avoid the unmentionable. Or perhaps they were devising a plan that would shake my faith, that would force me to move from our home, that would dispose of the 'Dorricks' and take the name that they themselves had adopted, whatever that was. But being Dorricks was the only name I was sure of. To say nothing of the betrayal that discarding that name would imply. I so convinced myself of their strategy, that I worked myself up into a rage and I had to sit on my bed for a while to calm myself. But if my boys had a strategy in mind, I too had a purpose to fulfil. I had to persuade them to visit their father, but I had little hope of succeeding.

They complimented me on my get-up. I had put on my best and they took my arms between them and hurried me gently to their car. I saw some net curtains stirring, but, unlike my boys, I was proud and delighted. Matthew drove and Martin sat beside him. I spread myself comfortably on the back seat. We drove wordlessly for a good ten minutes until the silence became embarrassing. I felt it wasn't my place to break it. Yet I did.

'It's been almost a year since I've seen you,' I said. As the words left my mouth, I felt the heavy weight of them, laced as they were with accusation. And though I meant every syllable of them, I regretted their sound. My boys made no response. Neither did I expect one, for how on earth could they answer but with a similarly loaded reply?

'We're going to a French restaurant,' Martin said, breaking yet another silence.

'That's nice,' I said, because I had to say something, but, in truth, I was indifferent to any cuisine, because my appetite was fast fading. I tried to cheer myself up and be grateful for their visit and their concern, even though it might all come to nothing.

We drew up at an hotel and an attendant approached the car.

'Good morning, Mr Davies,' I heard the man say as he opened the driver's door. 'It's good to see you again.'

It was the first time I'd heard of my boys' new patronym and I noted that at least they had retained the same initial.

My boys were obviously regulars at the place and were made welcome. They introduced me as their mother. That was safe enough for them I thought, until the man said, 'Welcome, Mrs Davies. I hope you enjoy your lunch.'

He stepped into the car and drove it away, leaving the three of us on the steps of the hotel. Three impostors and I felt ashamed for us all.

The boys took my arms once more, though less hurriedly this time. No Dorricks associates were likely to be found in this quarter. It was a grand dining room, overlooking the river and they had chosen a perfect table from which one could view the river traffic chugging along in its unconcerned way. When we were seated, a waiter approached and presented me with a rose corsage. 'Happy birthday, Mrs Davies,' he said. I smiled at him. My spirits lifted and I thanked the boys who had clearly gone to much trouble to make it a day I would remember. My appetite returned and I was prepared to sit silently throughout the whole meal in order to show my gratitude. And I kept that promise to myself through the first course of smoked salmon and blinis. Apart from comments on the food and its presentation, none of those stifled words were spoken. But gratitude is not durable. It is banal to start with, and as far as I was concerned it had run its course. And by the time the main dish had arrived, the words began to itch and threatened to choke me. So I opened my mouth on them, if only to free an air passage, and I mentioned the word that was strangling us all.

'Your father,' I said. And stopped. They were staring at me.

'What about him?' Martin's tone was cold.

'He's innocent,' I said.

A glance of pity passed between them, as if their mother was out of her mind.

'We don't want to talk about it,' Matthew said.

'But I do.' My voice was raised. I didn't care that the diners at the neighbouring tables pretended not to eavesdrop. 'I visit him as often as I'm allowed. In prison,' I added. I wanted to put the other diners fully in the picture.

'Shush, Mother,' Matthew said. He was blushing with shame.

But I didn't care about that. It was the 'Mother' appellation that stopped me in my tracks. Where had that refined word come from? I had always been 'Mum' to them and 'Mummy' in their infant years. But never 'Mother'. That word belonged to another class, a class that didn't harbour a prisoner in its midst, a class of virtue, wealth and propriety, and no doubt the class which my apostate children had joined. I was sickened by the word, and angry, and that anger fuelled the words that were to follow. No more gratitude. I was going to give them what for.

'Each time I visit him,' I went on, 'he asks after you. He asks *for* you. He wonders why you don't visit him.'

Then out came the words that they had not meant to utter. Words that they had tried to muzzle in the hope that they would not be called for.

'We don't want anything to do with him,' Matthew said.

'That's right,' came from Martin. 'We don't want to be known as his children. Ever again.'

I felt a lump in my throat and I took a gulp of wine to swallow it. Then another. And another. I considered that my only escape from the pain was in alcohol and I stretched out my glass for a refill. Matthew looked at Martin who nodded, then he called over the wine waiter and ordered another bottle. Both hoped that the drink would soothe me, but feared too that I would shame them.

'He was a good father to you,' I persisted. 'Do you remember how he used to play with you on the sands? The castles he made for you? The moats? The turrets? And how every weekend, he played cricket or football with you? How could you forget all that?'

'All that was before it happened,' Martin said. 'Please Mother,' he added, 'finish your steak.'

'Stop calling me that,' I said. I would have yelled at him, but the alcohol served as a mute and my gentle voice offended me. 'If you must address me, Mum will do. As it always has done.'

'Then finish your steak, Mum,' Martin said, and he managed a smile. But my appetite had ebbed, and I placed my knife and fork together on my plate.

'What would you like to do this afternoon?' Matthew asked. 'We could go to the zoo, if you like. You always enjoyed that.'

They were desperate to change the subject but I would not let them get away so easily.

'He wants you to visit him,' I insisted. 'You owe him at least that.'

They were silent.

'I'm begging you,' I said.

'Stop it, Mum.' Martin put his hand on mine. 'We know that he did those things. We don't know why. Nobody ever will. But we know that he is guilty. He almost said so himself. And we can't live with it, Matthew and I. It happened in another place and in another time. We want nothing to do with it.'

'But we want to keep in touch with you,' Matthew said.

71

'You mean once a year? On my birthday? That kind of keeping in touch?'

'We'll make it more often,' Martin said.

It sounded as if they were doing me a favour, and I was moved to assert myself. If they refused to see Donald, then out of loyalty I had to refuse to see them as well.

'I don't want to keep in touch,' I said. 'Not even on birthdays. You left me alone when I needed you most. I let you go without complaint. But now I can do without you and your birthday support. If you don't visit your father, then I don't want you to visit me.'

I made to rise. I would find my own way home. The tears were gathering behind my eyes, and I feared a cloud-burst. I had to get out of that room before I exploded.

But as I rose, I heard the strains of 'Happy birthday' and through a blur of tears, I saw the approach of a large birthday cake, its token candles flaring. And the tears flooded. I could only hope that the waiters would consider me deeply moved by this display of affection. Tears of joy or despair look exactly the same so I let them flow, uncaring how they were read. Inside myself, I cursed the cake but I knew I had to gather strength to blow out those bloody candles. What little breath I had was busy masking my sobs.

They brought the trolley to a stop by the side of our table. And we had an audience too. All the other diners, happy birthdaying one who wished she had never been born.

'Take a deep breath now,' the head waiter advised.

I blew as hard as I could, but my breath would hardly have disturbed a feather.

'We'll help you,' the waiter said, and they all joined in, even my apostate sons; and the smoking, snuffed-out candles smelt like a funeral pyre.

I knew I could not leave, so I sat myself down again and accepted Matthew's handkerchief to dry my eyes. My sons knew they were not tears of joy.

'Eat the cake,' Matthew said gently. 'Then we'll take you home.'

So I cut and I shared and I sipped coffee and even a brandy until, in front of all the other diners, we could decently take our leave.

The homeward journey was silent all the way and none of us attempted to break that silence. The boys hurried me through my front door, and sat me down.

'We love you, Mum,' Martin said. 'The three of us can still be together.'

'Thank you for lunch and everything,' I said.

They seemed in no hurry to leave. But I was anxious for them to go. I wanted to be on my own. I would not crawl back into bed. The reality was a family destroyed. And I had to learn to face it.

THE DIARY

FIVE DOWN. FOUR TO GO.

I took some leave from my mission. I had to. I sensed a growing disgust with myself. My last encounter with Alistair Morris had thrown me a little. A man had gone to the police and confessed to the murder. I was outraged. He was treading on my crusade. His arrest was headlined in the papers. He was helping the police with their inquiries, the report said. A copper's euphemism for beating the shit out of him. Anyway, they released him after a few days, which was a relief. All that was over a year ago.

There was nothing special about Morris. It was just that he seemed so much part of a conveyor belt, almost inevitable. Murder was becoming a habit with me, so habitual that I was in danger of losing sight of its real purpose. I had failed to keep that aim in mind. And as that purpose dimmed, so did my conscience brighten. Itchingly. I prickled with self-reproach. But I'm glad to say that I felt no hint of remorse. And that saved me. I would never, but never, be sorry. My mission was just, and I kept its purpose in mind as the idle months rolled by. I made a picture of it, not that I was ever likely to forget it, but if one does nothing about it, the picture can blur. So I drew it in my mind, and varnished it so that it was sealed on my retina. A simple picture. Just an attic room. And a rope. I needed no more. A blink would not erase it. Neither would sleep. Never. Until my mission was fulfilled.

In time, I set about arranging my next sortie. It so happened that my boys were going to Amsterdam for a short break. They would be away for a week. Verry and I had not had a holiday alone for years and I suggested we take the train and spend a few days in Paris. Verry was excited and I booked the tickets and an hotel. And as I was making these arrangements, I had an outrageous idea. There was no reason why I shouldn't spread my net wide and at the same time give old Wilkins a treat. I'd send him continental.

My French wasn't bad. Enough to get by on introductions and statements of purpose. In any case, my crusade did not entail a great deal of conversation. I practised what I was going to say. My research uncovered Mademoiselle Lacroix, a psychotherapist who practised in the rue du Seine. I studied a map of Paris to familiarise myself with the area and by the time we were ready to leave, my preparations were complete. I would put off the doing of the deed until a few hours before our departure. I reckoned the time it would take a cab to travel from the rue du Seine to the Gare du Nord, with leeway for traffic jams. This one would have to be a quickie, I decided. I would use no disguise. Just gloves. As usual. In and out. One, two and Bob's your uncle. Or rather, *Robert est votre oncle.*

Verry was very excited. Tourist excited. And so was I. But for different reasons. I could have done without the Eiffel Tower and Les Invalides and the Louvre. I was mission excited. My crusade was once again under way.

We did the tourist bits, Verry and I, and we walked a lot. I manoeuvred one of our walks to go down the rue du Seine. I paused at my chosen door, ostensibly to tie my shoelace, and in so doing, I noted that my quarry lived on the ground floor, a fact which pleased me. On the day of our departure, I deposited Verry in a coffee house near the rue du Seine and I told her that I wanted to browse in a bookshop near by. She was happy to rest her feet and I ordered her a coffee and a brioche. She is so agreeable, my Verry. I could easily have told her I was going to Devon.

I strolled over to the site of my next quarry, putting on my gloves as I did so, holding the string at the ready. At her door, I did not hesitate. I rang the bell and prayed that she was at home. I waited, but not for long. She herself opened it. Or rather, I presumed it was she. But I had to make sure. I couldn't sully my crusade with the wrong number.

'Mademoiselle Lacroix?' I asked.

'*Oui*,' she said.

I was unnerved to find her rather young and beautiful, but I imaged that picture of mine in the attic, and all scruple faded.

'*Qu'est-ce que vous voulez?*' she asked.

My French dried, but I didn't care. I didn't need words in any language. I simply pushed past her, closed the door, and measured her French neck with my string. I prayed that no one would come in or go out and I allowed her backward fall, felt her dying pulse and shut the door on her, rather as I had left poor Miss Mayling on the hall floor.

Verry had finished her coffee, and I paid the bill and hailed a cab. Once on the train, I breathed freely and welcomed the old elation, that normal after-taste of my mission. I had a sudden surge of love for Verry, and I decided that on our return home, I'd give her a good seeing to. So,

FIVE DOWN. FOUR TO GO.

Wilkins was idling at his desk. It was over a year now, and no further psychotherapist had been murdered. Perhaps the killer had died? Or done the decent thing, out of shame? And just as he was placing the whole shrink she-bang on the back-burner, he had news that the killer, no longer deceased or a suicide, had struck again.

'Shit,' he said.

Now Wilkins did not favour bad language, but he cursed the killer who had risen as if from the dead. But worse than that: he had spread his net wide. And God knows how much wider. Still, a trip to the scene of the crime was not something to be scoffed at. He had never been on Eurostar, and only once to Paris when he was a boy. He'd gone over on the ferry, and had been seasick all the way. The train would be smooth and an adventure. He tried not to appear too excited. He was glad that the responsibility of an arrest would now be shared, and that the gendarmes would have to get their fingers out. But from his weary experience, Wilkins had little hope of finding any clues, and if this latest killing had taken place on his home ground, he wondered whether, in his helplessness, he would have bothered to go at all. But he fitted himself out in a new suit, thinking that Paris ruled the world of fashion, and with the local French detective, who mercifully spoke very good English, he made his way to the rue du Seine.

The French detective had already visited the apartment and confirmed what Wilkins could have told him, sight unseen. Garrotting, guitar string, no prints, no forced entry.

And, unsurprisingly, no witnesses. There were too many people in the street at the time. Man or woman or even child: it could have been anybody.

There was little that Wilkins could do in Paris. He had to leave the investigation to his opposite number. But while he was in the city, he decided to savour its delights. However, one night of those delights frightened him and he fled back in the train to his decent semi in the suburbs. He wondered where the killer would strike next. There was now no stopping him and despite his despondency, it was an exciting prospect. He had a favourite cousin in Geneva whom he hadn't seen for years. Geneva must be riddled with psychotherapists, he thought. But it was a lottery. The luck of the draw. There was no obvious pattern to the killer's choice of location. Only the target was constant. So the next one, and Wilkins was sure there would be another, and others too, the next one could be anywhere.

Donald's been moved again. They said it was for his own safety. He'd been attacked, they informed me, though his injuries were not serious.

I couldn't understand it. Donald was not a prime target. It was not as if he were a child abuser. And in any case he is innocent. Though nobody will believe him. Except me, of course. What else dare I believe?

He's been transferred to Parkhurst prison on the Isle of Wight. Although it was a long way from London, and necessitated a ferry crossing, I looked forward to my next visit. I love the sea and although it's only across the Solent, you can imagine that you're travelling abroad. But Parkhurst has an ominous ring. Only Category A prisoners are housed there, and since it is an island there's no possibility of escape. Not that my Donald would ever try it. It would make him look guilty and he wouldn't have any of that. When I think of Parkhurst, I think of Alcatraz and the birdman. I saw a film about it once. My Donald won't be a birdman, but he'll be the Painter of Parkhurst. They might even make a film about him. Silly, isn't it, the way I'm thinking? But I'm trying to put out of my mind a letter I had this morning. It's not bad news, but it means that I have to make a decision. An important one. And I'm not good at decisions. Donald always made them for me. Trouble is, it's about Donald and his business and I've got to make a decision on his behalf. It's almost a month till my next visiting permit and these people want an answer straight away. It's about his offices.

He'd paid the rent in advance. A whole year of it. And it's due again next week. The owners want to know if, in the circumstances – that's their phrase – I want to renew it. And if not, I must give written notice and clear the place of all furniture and effects within two weeks. I know it would be foolish to keep up with the rent, but giving it up seems to be giving up on Donald; seems to assume he'll never be free to start his business again. Moreover, I would be invading his privacy. I had never set foot in his office. He had always insisted it was his place, and his alone. And I would have to go through his papers too, in case there was something important he'd left unattended. It would be like prying. Still, it had to be done. So I stopped thinking about the Painter of Parkhurst and the film that they would make of him, and I wrote to the office landlords cancelling the contract and assuring them that I would have the place cleared.

I thought I would do it straight away and get it over with. I would not tell my boys. They would regard it as a sign of my surrender; that at last I was beginning to see sense. They had been in touch a few times since my birthday, asking me out to the theatre and lunches and so on. But their refusal to visit Donald still rankled and I wanted to let them know it.

The letter gave the address of the office. I didn't even know that. Donald's bunch of keys still lay on the hall table where he always left them. I took them with me. One of them would fit. I had no idea what I would find there. I'd heard that the police had stripped it after his arrest. I suspected that there would be some furniture that I would have to get rid of and I hoped that would be all, because I didn't want to make any troublesome discoveries.

The first key I selected from the bunch fitted exactly, thus giving me no excuse to delay my entry. I opened the door gingerly, as if I expected to find someone inside. And, indeed, I did call out Donald's name and wondered whether I was in my right mind. He occupied only one room in the building and that was a relief. As was the paucity of its furnishings. Just one desk, two chairs and a filing cabinet. I tried the phone and found it disconnected. The furniture, such as it was, was old and scuffed. Unsaleable. I would have to pay someone to take it away. Having made that decision, I wanted to leave but I felt obliged to examine the desk drawers and those of the filing cabinet before I could honestly tell myself that I had done a thorough job. So far I had discovered nothing to trouble me. Simply entering Donald's office and viewing a few sticks of furniture was no invasion of privacy. But going through his drawers was another matter. I sat on one of the rickety chairs, and considered whether should there be any sleeping dogs I ought to let them lie. But I confess that, despite my scruples, I was also tempted. Tempted to discover something that would throw some light on all that had happened and equally terrified of such a discovery. But I considered that the police had rifled the place, and taken away anything that could be evidence, so I felt safe in opening the first drawer of the desk. Then the second and the third and the three on the other side and all, apart from a few rubber bands and paper clips, were empty. So it was with a certain confidence that I moved to the filing cabinet. Six drawers in all. And all mercifully empty.

I left the office satisfied. On Donald's release, he could set up elsewhere.

On my way home, I had a happy moment. They happen sometimes. Rarely, and they don't last. But it's a moment one remembers for a long time, a moment that one never understands. I began to look forward to my next visit, to the crossing over the water. I could pretend I was going abroad to a country where the Painter of Parkhurst would be waiting to meet me. I gave a thought to my boys and I wondered whether the sea trip would tempt them. But they were city boys now, restaurant boys, futures and dividend boys. The only ferry that would lure them would be to an exotic island. They would find the Solent faintly insulting.

'Bugger them,' I said to myself, as I recalled that brief moment of happiness. 'It's their loss as well as Donald's. But for the latter, I mourned. I would try yet again, I decided. When they next asked me out, I would go with them and make a thorough nuisance of myself.

But thinking badly of my boys did not please me, and when I reached home I decided to comfort myself by looking through my photograph albums and view them once again as children. In Margate, on the sands, and in better times. I kept the album in my underwear drawer. The police had rifled that too but they seemed uninterested in seaside snaps and they had left them for my comfort. I remember feeling deeply grateful. I sat on my bed with the book on my lap, and page by page, and under the sun and in the water and on the sands, I relished our stainless past. I noted how the boys grew over the years, how the donkey rides gave way to coconut shies and the fairground. And even a rifle range with Donald clutching a lone goldfish in a polythene bag. Happy times. The last page of the album was devoted to a family portrait taken by a photographer on the pier. And tucked into the back flap, unframed, were the boys' certificates: silver for swimming, distinction for elocution, and stars for English and maths. And I was proud of them again.

As I was closing the album, I noticed that three small pieces of paper had been clipped to the maths certificate. I hadn't noticed them before but it was a long time since I had looked at the album. The last time Donald had been with me and we had looked and laughed at it together. I was curious and I unclipped them. They were three receipts. All were from a funeral director in north London, acknowledging the payment of interment expenses. I noted the dates of the first two. Almost a year apart. I surmised that they referred to Donald's parents. I recalled the funerals he told me he had attended. But the last receipt was a puzzle. It was dated from before Donald and I had met. It confirmed Donald's collection of an urn of ashes. Whose ashes they were was not referred to, simply that Donald was the collector. I thought perhaps that the ashes had been those of an aunt or an uncle. Or they could have been those of a friend. But I doubted that. Donald had since told me that he'd never had a friend. It was a puzzle all right. I wondered why Donald had put them there. Surely he must have meant for me to discover them. His way of telling me something. But what? He had left me clues, but without any guidance at all.

I sensed I didn't want to know any further. I certainly would not question Donald on my next visit. Indeed I would not even mention the office or the cancellation of his tenancy. Whether he was innocent or guilty, I didn't want my doubts fed or my certainty threatened. I would let matters lie.

THE DIARY

STILL FIVE DOWN. FOUR TO GO.

After Paris I had to take a break. Paris. I must have been out of my mind! The risks I took. But by God, it was well worth it. Paris refreshed my spirits, and I'm not referring to the Eiffel Tower or the Louvre. Just that brief encounter on the rue du Seine. It restored my faith in my mission. But I knew that nothing could top that Paris trip, so I had to lie low for a while until the elation was distilled.

I followed the newspaper accounts with diligence. Every one of them. I even bought copies of *Le Monde* to acquaint myself with the French version of events. All reported the absence of clues. *Impasse.* And all concluded, in both the English and French papers, that the murder of poor Mademoiselle Lacroix was a copy-cat, and had nothing to do with the serial murder in England. I was not in the least offended by this. On the contrary, this conclusion could lead to other imitations and it signalled that any psychotherapist, anywhere in the world, was at risk. And such a thought warmed the cockles of my heart. But it's still five down and four to go. Time to recapitulate.

Harry Winston. The good man. But good or bad, his profession qualified him for dispatch. Angela Mayling. An easy prey, a death probably unmourned, but that was no business of mine. Then the Barry Island lady, Bronwen Hughes, who saw through my petticoats and had the temerity to analyse me. So good riddance to bad rubbish. After the Welsh woman, it was back to London and Alistair Morris. He too saw through my disguise, and it was not good for him. And now we come to the best of all. Mademoiselle Lacroix of rue du Seine. The so-called copy-cat murder. The fastest and the most exhilarating of all. It's no wonder I need a break from my mission.

Since my Paris adventure, I've taken to reading newspapers. I'm not too busy at the office, and until I am ready for my next mission it helps to pass the time. The papers are full of terrible stories. Muggings, thuggery, rape and murder. Even the political reports are coloured with the same lurid hues. But one particular story caught my eye, pertaining as it did to my own personal crusade. A young woman, in her early twenties, from a wealthy family, living in Liverpool, had fallen into a deep depression. Parental treats and overseas holidays had done little to lift her spirits. The family doctor, lacking confidence in anti-depressants, recommended psychotherapy. He should have known better. The girl's father forked out the payments, which, over three years at five sessions a week, amounted to a very tidy sum. During her sessions, the girl was encouraged to explore her childhood and after much prodding and suggestion she was seduced into recalling the fact that her father had sexually abused her. It's more than possible that the therapist had herself or himself been similarly abused in childhood and was going to make bloody sure that every father in the land had done the same. The patient was now furnished with the positive cause of her depression and thus armed, she confronted her father, the man who had footed the bill for his own ruin. Under the daughter's accusations, her mother suffered a nervous breakdown. But her father, innocent and broken, drove to the nearest coast and walked into the sea. He had virtually financed his own execution.

I wish I could ferret out the name of that therapist. He or she would be a more than fitting target for my crusade. But no doubt they are legion. False memory syndrome seems to be the 'in' thing nowadays, and though my mission is strictly personal, I like to think that it is also on behalf of all those families that have been destroyed by false accusation of any kind.

You would think that that story would have urged me on with my crusade, but the after-effects of Paris still lingered and I had first to simmer down, lest I should involuntarily put myself at risk. So, it's

STILL FIVE DOWN. FOUR TO GO.

Wilkins was uneasy. Although most were of the opinion, both in Paris and in London, that the killing of Mademoiselle Lacroix was a copy-cat deed, he was not swayed. It was too skilled a murder for an amateur one-off. Amateurs tended to leave clues. But the Paris incident had been in every particular exactly like each of the shrink murders to date. And there was no doubt in his mind that whoever had committed them was one and the same as the Paris killer. He continued to keep in touch with his opposite number in Paris who took no care to hide his irritation at his interference. As far as he was concerned the Lacroix murder was a matter for the French police and they were getting on with it. Apparently they had interviewed a number of witnesses and were holding at least four suspects in custody. But Wilkins knew it was all a show. The French had to be seen to be doing something. Wilkins smiled over the telephone and said he would continue to keep in touch.

Once again, he studied the files relating to the previous murders, and he consulted Dr Arbuthnot regarding the Paris affair. But that Mr Know-all tended to agree with the French. It was a copy-cat business and had nothing to do with the English cases, but he warned that it might well lead to others of its kind. Wilkins decided that thereafter he would bypass Dr Arbuthnot and his opinions and he went back to his files. But studying them over and over again revealed no more clues than the killer himself had left. It had been over a year since the killer had struck. He had never waited that long. His fingers must have itched on that guitar string. Itched so persistently, that he simply had to perform. And this compulsion entailed excitement and risk. Both fulfillable in the trip to Paris.

And then Wilkins hit upon an idea. It was a shot in the dark, but it might pay off. He had no idea when the killer had travelled to Paris or indeed by what means. But he was pretty sure that the wanted man had left the city immediately after the murder. And probably by Eurostar, since it was the quickest and least encumbered way to leave. So he acquired a passenger list of the return trains for that day. And the same from the airlines. He received over two thousand names. But he was not disconcerted. He reckoned he could discount all family parties, and all men accompanied by wives or partners. This was a job of a loner who would hardly take a partner in tow. So out of these lists he selected the names of those men who had travelled alone. And mercifully there were comparatively few. Wilkins ordered his men to ferret them out and then to bring them in for questioning, assuring them that they were simply needed for elimination. He himself would interview them personally and in the police station of whatever town they resided in. Thus Wilkins found himself travelling the length and breadth of the country. But it did not trouble him. He was not happy with the relegation of the therapist killings. In his mind, Paris had once more put the pot back on the boil. And he was about to stir it with his old relish.

Many of the lone travellers came from London. He kept them till last, suspecting they might prove more fruitful. Birmingham and its half-dozen travellers was his first port of call. He was given a room in the central police station, and he interviewed them all, one by one. All of them were more than willing to help. But Wilkins had never been fooled by willingness. He viewed any mateyness with the Force with a faint suspicion. All of them had been on business in the city or the countryside. They all gave names and addresses of companies they had visited as proof. They travelled in wine, textiles, ceramics. One had gone to visit his ailing mother in Provence. The interviews yielded nothing. Then he went off to Manchester and a similar reception.

Wilkins rested his hopes on London, though by the time he came back to the capital, his confidence had waned and he decided that none of those who had come forward was worth pursuing. Neither were those whom he interviewed in London. All were willing to be interviewed and gave proof of their alibis. All were believable. There was just one more lone traveller to investigate, a Mr Coleman, and when he entered the interviewing room, he seemed to epitomise the total folly of Wilkins' hopeful shot in the dark, for he had one leg and moved slowly on crutches. Wilkins saw no point at all in questioning him, but he felt the man would be offended if he didn't. So he invited him to sit down, which Mr Coleman did. Slowly and with a smile.

He was a handsome man, somewhere in his fifties, Wilkins guessed. But the smile worried him. There was, after all, nothing to smile about. A young French woman had been cruelly garrotted on her doorstep. Mr Coleman's smile might have been that of a villain.

Wilkins began with the usual question. 'What were you doing in Paris, Mr Coleman?' he asked.

'I can't tell you,' Mr Coleman said. 'It's a secret.'

Wilkins leaned forward in his chair. He sensed a fruitful moment.

'What passes between us,' he said, 'is in absolute confidence. I need to know why you were in Paris. I need to eliminate you from our inquiries.'

Mr Coleman hesitated and his smile dissolved. 'My wife would never forgive me,' he said.

'She need never know,' Wilkins said, having a pretty shrewd idea of what Mr Coleman had been up to.

Mr Coleman leaned forward in his chair. 'Are you sure this won't go any further?' he asked.

Wilkins nodded. 'Just between you and me.'

Then Mr Coleman seemed happy enough to open his heart.

'I go there about once a month,' he said. 'I've been doing so for about ten years. I tell my wife I go to keep in touch with the galleries and what's happening in modern art. She's not interested in that sort of thing. And I *do* go to the galleries. That part of it is true. But I go with my friend. She's a painter. That's how I met her. In a gallery, ten years ago. She's an abstract painter, you know, and she's quite successful. Only last week she sold two pictures.'

Wilkins shifted in his chair. He was not prepared to listen to the progress of Mr Coleman's mistress. He suspected that the man would have happily sat there the whole day, detailing his adulterous affair simply because he had no one else to tell it to.

'What's her name?' he interrupted. 'And what's her address?'

'Is that absolutely necessary?' Mr Coleman asked.

'It's part of the procedure,' Wilkins said. 'I repeat, it's totally confidential.'

Mr Coleman took a notepad out of his pocket, tore out a page and wrote down the information that was requested. It was as if he suspected that walls have ears.

Wilkins glanced at the note and pocketed it. He thought about his wife and tried to imagine his own infidelity. And he shuddered with a mixture of excitement and disgust. He was anxious to get rid of Mr Coleman. He had no appetite for further confidences. He rose from his chair.

'Thank you, Mr Coleman,' he said. 'That will be all.'

Mr Coleman rose reluctantly from his seat. He was disappointed. He had looked forward to a one-sided chinwag. Man to man. He knew no one in whom he could confide. And in sworn secrecy. He comforted himself with the thought of his next Paris rendezvous.

But Wilkins had little to comfort himself with. His long shot had been far too long to pay off and at the station they might well be laughing behind his back. Yet he could not dismiss the possibility of a link between the Paris murder and the others. It wasn't just a hunch. He felt it in his bones. The killer of them all was the same man.

I'd had a letter from the prison. It was friendly and I was grateful for that. It informed me of the best way to travel there. Portsmouth to Fishbourne and then a special bus. I didn't like the special bus bit. On the train and the ferry, I could be anybody. But the bus would mark me as a prison visitor and although I knew that my Donald was innocent, I didn't want to publicise my visit. For my second visit, I would have to work out a less conspicuous way of getting there. The letter also gave a list of items that could be brought into the prison and those that were forbidden. Food of any kind came into the latter category but games were allowed, such as playing cards and chess sets. I was disappointed. I'd wanted to bake Donald his favourite sponge cake. I didn't know what to take him. He didn't play chess or cards. My Donald had no hobbies. He flew a kite sometimes on the common, but a kite would be pretty pointless in Parkhurst. Yet I couldn't go empty-handed. Then I remembered that he'd started to paint, so I bought him a paintbox, with two good brushes. It was better than nothing. Although I was excited at the prospect of a visit, and of crossing the water to boot, I was nervous. I couldn't think of anything to talk about. I was too loaded with subjects unmentionable. Emma was one of them. I didn't think he'd want to be reminded of her. The boys were another. I could not tell him of their refusal. And that receipt for the ashes. That above all. I could never mention that. God knows where it might lead. He would have no news to give me, so he would naturally ask for news from home and since my life was uneventful I would have to invent news, so on the train down to Portsmouth I cobbled together a few stories about the neighbours and their troubles. Terrible troubles. There was no way I was going to impart good news about anybody. Not while my Donald was suffering. So I invented fatal accidents, bankruptcies, even suicides. I hoped they would comfort him, as, I must confess, they surely comforted me.

The Portsmouth train station led directly to the ferry. I boarded it and climbed straight on to the top deck and leaned over the railings with the free wind on my face and the roar of the engines in my ears. I tried to clear my mind of any thoughts. I wanted to enjoy myself, and my kind of thoughts would have been an impediment to any fun. I stayed at the rail for some time, but it grew too cold for comfort, so I went downstairs to the bar and bought myself a large brandy. I'm not much of a drinker, but I thought it would give me courage. I was more than nervous. I was frightened. I feared what I would find. Parkhurst was known to be no picnic, and I was afraid that Donald might be ill or thoroughly depressed. But I would put on a happy face. I hoped I could touch him, kiss him even, but I expected a barrier and I prayed it would be a glass one with a telephone, so that at least we could play our game.

I sipped my brandy and enjoyed it. The bar area of the ferry was full, and there were few unoccupied tables. I felt ashamed sitting at one all on my own, so when a woman, carrying her glass, approached I motioned her to take a seat at my table, and we naturally fell into conversation. She asked me if I lived on the island. I told her I had friends there and I was going to visit them. I hoped she would not enquire as to details. So, quickly, I asked her the same.

She too had friends there, she said, whom she was going to visit. We were silent then. It seemed that neither of us was interested in further exploration. I wondered if, like me, she was lying. A good liar can smell another, and I sensed that each of us would dodge the Parkhurst bus until the other was out of sight.

'My name's Mary,' she said. 'Mary Comley.'

I felt obliged to give her mine, but as you already know I have problems with my Christian name, but even more with the Dorricks and especially on this journey and where it must inevitably lead. For Dorricks is a well-known name, and a hated name and that name alone would give the lie to my so-called friends on the island.

'Joan,' I said, once more trying that name that allowed for no variation and 'Jones,' I added, off the top of my head. I put the two names together in my mind. Joan Jones. It sounded so preposterous, it just had to be true.

'I'm Welsh,' I said, as if that explained everything.

'I'm pleased to meet you, Mrs Jones,' Mrs Comley – if that was her real name – said.

I held out my hand and said, 'Likewise.'

Again there was silence between us. I was anxious for the ferry to dock, for any further conversation between us would have entailed more and more lies and I was fast running out of invention. I sensed that Mrs Comley was restive too, and probably for the same reason.

'It's going to be a fine day,' she said, looking out of the window. 'Not a cloud in the sky.'

We were on safe ground at last. The weather. You couldn't lie about that one. It spoke for itself. But once spoken, it could not be elaborated on. So again there was silence, broken at last by the voice on the tannoy asking car owners to return to their vehicles. We were about to land.

Mrs Comley rose quickly. I think she wanted to be one of the first to get away so that she could lose no time with her 'friends'. I said goodbye to her and wished her a good stay. I tarried a while, sipping my brandy and I was among the last to leave the ferry. I did not fear missing the bus. It would wait for me. My name was on the passenger list. I went down the stairs to the lower decks, and walked through the pedestrian gangway as the last cars were leaving. The bus was standing at the dockside. It had no markings and that was a relief. I went towards it, looking behind me to my right and left, as if I were being followed. I did not want to be seen boarding the bus, so I passed it by nonchalantly, then darted back to the open door and rushed inside. There was lots of room, but I did not take a window seat. I sat at the back, in the middle of the bench, and kept my head down. I heard the start of the engine, but still we idled.

'Hurry along now,' I heard the conductor say, and I looked up to see him help a woman on to the bus and the doors close after her. She hung her head as she walked down the aisle, then raised it to find a seat.

Mrs Comley. We stared at each other, and to my relief, she shrugged her shoulders and smiled. I tapped the empty seat next to mine and she joined me.

'It's not our fault,' she said, as she settled herself down.

It had never occurred to me that I was guilty of Donald's incarceration. I believed he was innocent, and that made me innocent too. Since it was now all out in the open, and it was clear that neither of us had island friends to visit, certain questions were permissible.

'Who are you visiting?' I asked.

'My husband,' she said. 'And you?'

'My husband too,' I told her.

'Mine's innocent,' she said.

I said nothing. I didn't want Donald's innocence to be classed with Mr Comley's. I was curious as to why he was in prison. I assumed it was for something quite major. One wasn't put in Parkhurst for stealing a packet of chewing gum. But that was a question one couldn't ask.

Mrs Comley must have read my mind. 'He's in for murder,' she said.

'So's mine,' I gladly volunteered. I was strangely pleased that we both had something in common.

'This your first time?' she asked.

'First time here,' I said. 'Donald's just been moved.' I was becoming familiar. Why not? I thought. We had much to share.

Mary responded. 'Steve's been here for four years. Six in Strangeways. He'll be up for parole soon.'

So he's already served ten years. He must be a lifer, I thought.

I had to respond. 'This is only Donald's second year.' I felt very low. Mrs Comley was far better off than I.

'I'm his only visitor,' she was saying. 'His family want nothing to do with him.'

'Neither do Donald's,' I said. I thought of my boys, but without affection. Rather with a deep resentment that I had to bear the burden alone. For that's what Donald had become. A burden, and one that I could never shake off. He was my life sentence. And I was innocent. But this was no time for resentment. I had to wear a happy face, one without a trace of blame. I had to tell him the fictitious news from home. I wanted to see his face light up at other people's troubles and I just prayed he wouldn't ask after the boys.

The bus stopped at the prison gates.

'Come on, dear,' Mrs Comley said. 'I'll show you the way.'

I followed her into the building and when asked, I whispered my real name. And I overheard hers, as she confessed to Mrs Cox. I put Stephen and Cox together. It was a name, in its time, as known and hated as Dorricks. I recalled him as the axe killer of his mother-in-law. And here was that poor victim's daughter visiting her mother's murderer. I didn't know how to construe it. Loyalty, perhaps? Punishment even? Or sheer weakness? And I realised that any of those motives could have applied to me.

They searched my handbag and little parcels before letting me through, and I followed Mrs Cox to the waiting room and sat beside her.

'We have to wait for the bell,' she said.

When it rang, she was the first to rise and I followed her along with all the others to the visitors room. No telephones, no glass partitions. Just a large open room, scattered with tables. I was disappointed. I would have preferred the distance. I didn't want a cuddle or a peck on the cheek or an hour of hand-holding. I saw him sitting at one of the tables, and when he saw me he rose. I wanted to run away, but I put on my smile and went towards him, and with every step I took I decided never, but never, to visit him again. I would go and live near my boys, change my name as they had done, and never mention Dorricks again. And with this resolve, I reached his table and suffered his cuddle, his kiss and his desperate holding of my hand.

I sat down beside him. I chose my place deliberately. I did not want to look him in the face as I would have been forced to do had I sat opposite him. But I did make myself look at him as I sat down and, for the first time since he had been arrested, I said to myself, 'My Donald is guilty.'

He wouldn't let go of me. He clung. I couldn't bear his touch but I suffered it, comforting myself with the thought that I would never have to suffer it again. I don't know what it was that had so changed me. Perhaps I was tired of all the lies, of the Comley/Cox pretence, of the Jones/Dorricks facade. But above all, tired of that phrase out of my own and Mrs Cox's mouth. 'He is innocent.' I was tired of it all.

'I am innocent,' was the first thing he said to me. 'You believe that, don't you, sweetheart?'

I nodded. What else could I do? He was looking well – even merry. And I was glad of it. It would have been hard to desert a man who was plainly in ill health and misery.

'You look well, Donald,' I said.

'And you too, Verry.'

The use of my name, that troublesome name, slightly shook my resolve. Only Donald could say it with such certainty, and with such affection. I smiled at him.

'I've waited so long for this visit,' he was saying. 'I've brought some of my paintings to show you.'

And then the Painter of Parkhurst flashed through my mind, and the film that they would make in Hollywood and my Donald on parole by public request. And slowly my resolve evaporated. All that remained was pity. A life sentence of pity, that no amount of counselling could conquer or assuage.

'What's it like here?' I asked.

'Not too bad,' he said. 'I've made some friends.'

That was a bonus, I thought. He'd made no friends on

the outside. What with friends and painting, prison might be the making of him, I thought, and that cheered me up a little. He did not ask for news from outside. He was too intent on showing me his paintings. Their content surprised me, for none of them depicted the prison or prison life. They were seascapes, reminiscent of our early holidays with the boys. And they were beautiful. And full of longing. They moved me unutterably, but served only to swell my pity. I praised them fulsomely. My Donald had at last found his voice, that voice so monosyllabic on the outside. It was as if he had at last found peace. And who was I to pity him? But pity, I knew, had nothing to do with his circum-stances. Pity was *my* need and, *faute de mieux*, pity was the only way I could stomach his incarceration.

'I painted this one especially for you,' he said. 'Not that I need any reminder of you, but it's as if you are here by my side.' He drew a sheet from underneath the pile and he laid it before me like an offering. It was a portrait of myself, painted by and from the heart. The likeness was astonishing, and though it was a fine portrayal in every particular, I had an acute sensation of being blackmailed. But I could not help but admire it. I told him it showed great talent and that I was very flattered. That seemed to please him.

'Encouragement helps,' he said, and as he was tidying up the sheets, I looked around at the other convicts and their visitors.

Mrs Cox stood out among them, partly because she was on her feet and seemed to be in a bit of a temper. I could not hear what she was saying, because she was hissing, as if fire was coming out of her mouth.

Others turned to look at her, and her husband cringed

with embarrassment. Then suddenly she turned and stormed out of the room, though there was a good half-hour left of visiting time. Poor Mr Cox. He made no move to follow her. He laid his head on the table, accepting defeat, and I wondered if Mrs Cox had fled the room with pity in her heels.

My Donald hadn't seemed to notice the disturbance and I thought I ought to bring it to his attention.

'Oh, we get a lot of that,' he said. 'Relatives get upset. And so do inmates, when they visit. But she'll be back next time. They always have a dust-up, I'm told, those two.'

'But why?' I dared to ask.

'He keeps saying he's innocent, and she only pretends to believe him. Not like you, Verry,' he said. 'You believe me, don't you? You know I'm innocent.'

I nodded my head. What else could I do? I was in a quandary. I wasn't convinced of his innocence, never had been, but at the same time, I couldn't believe that he was guilty. In view of our years together, the happiness we'd shared, it was much easier to presume his innocence, whatever the opinions of twelve men and women true. My former resolve was now totally shaken and I leaned forward and kissed him on the cheek, knowing that I would visit again and again and again, until he was exonerated. Even so, as I was kissing him, I sensed that I was out of my mind.

The remainder of visiting time passed easily and he seemed almost relieved when it was over. He told me he wanted to get back to his painting. 'It's my life-line,' he said. 'That and your visits.'

Again I felt faintly blackmailed, but I kissed him and told him that he was a fine painter. Once more I thought of

Alcatraz and Hollywood and as I left the room, waving, I realised that my former resolve had been a hiccup, and that I must never entertain such thoughts again.

Outside the prison, the bus was waiting and the visitors were already boarding. I looked around for Mrs Cox but there was no sign of her. So I boarded and made my way to the back of the bus. There she sat, huddled in the corner, weeping.

I put my arm around her. 'It's not easy,' I said.

'He's innocent,' she sobbed.

'Of course.' I comforted her. And comforted myself with our shared self-deception.

'But he killed my mother,' she went on.

Nothing added up. Nothing at all. All was confusion. Mrs Cox was indeed my soulmate. Neither of us dared to believe what was real, so we fashioned another kind of truth that was easier to accommodate. We had to. But it was not all that easy. And certainly not comfortable. For both Mrs Cox and I would be forever plagued with pity. And it was pity that would lace our stirrings in the small hours, a pity so dangerously close to resentment and anger that it led to a paralysing confusion.

THE DIARY

SIX DOWN. THREE TO GO.

Yes, I survived my Paris sortie and it was time I went back to work. Or rather, to my mission. In any case, Wilkins had had a long enough break. It was time for him to go back to work too.

Up till now I had gotten away with murder, to coin a phrase. My easy dispatch in Paris had made me cocky and I had to take a break for a while to steady myself. I was uneasy about killing women. But I knew that gender was irrelevant. Man or woman, it was the profession that was my target. Nevertheless, I chose a man for my next hit. A Dr James Fortescue. He sounded posh and learned, and although those factors did not whet my appetite, they lessened my scruples.

I had taken the trouble to do a little research on Dr Fortescue. I had an urge to know a little more of the figure that I was about to eliminate. It was totally unnecessary, of course. Dr Fortescue just had to be a psychotherapist – nothing more. But I thought that my previous dispatches had been too perfunctory, and I felt obliged to discover a little more about my victim than his or her mere profession.

Thus I discovered that Dr Fortescue was a therapist who practised according to Freudian methods. And among these was an interest in dreams. I decided to oblige him. I forget most of my dreams, but one sticks in my mind. Probably because I have it often. The same dream. The first time I dreamt it coincided with the beginning of my crusade. And from time to time it repeats itself. I myself don't understand it. So I proposed to throw it over Dr Fortescue's desk, to make of it what he would.

He lived alone on the edge of a London suburb, close to a famous public school. That gave me an idea. It's true I'm a man well into my forties but I have worn well and at a pinch I could be mistaken for a school-leaving prefect. I am tall and lean, and I can affect a gangling gait. So I took myself off to the school uniform department of a large store and on the pretence of buying for my son who was on holiday, I purchased a blazer, a tie and a cap of the relevant uniform colours. I dressed in my office, and I have to say that I could have fooled anybody. And if any witnesses came forward, they could only offer a schoolboy, which would in no way please Wilkins.

I was given a morning appointment, eight o'clock to be precise, and I marvelled at how these people beavered away from early morning till late at night in order to ruin and destroy.

I parked my car well away from Dr Fortescue's house. I was nervous as I walked towards it. I realised that I was out of practice. For murder is a skill that can rust if not continually exercised. In my mind, I rehearsed the usual moves as I fingered the string in my pocket. At his front door, I hesitated before ringing his bell. I knew that hesitation was dangerous so I rang it with some force, and many times. Dr Fortescue must have sensed an emergency for the door was immediately opened.

He was a kind-looking man, a father-figure, and I knew that this would not be an easy dispatch. He smiled at me, and that didn't help either. He motioned me to follow him.

'I wasn't expecting a schoolboy,' he said, as he led me into his office. 'You could have told the school to call me. I would have come.'

I didn't know what he was talking about. Normally, I would

have been happy to have fooled him, but I was sad that he was so taken in by my disguise. For a fatal moment I thought of leaving, of writing this one off. But it had already gone too far. Besides, together with my weapon, I had brought my dream.

He motioned me to sit down. 'Now what's troubling you?' he asked.

'I don't think it's important,' I began. 'It's probably nothing.'

'But it seems to be troubling you,' he said.

I nodded.

'Tell me about it. Perhaps I can help you.'

'Well,' I said, settling down, 'it's about a dream I keep having. It's a very sunny day in the dream. A splendid day. I'm about ten years old and I'm in a park. I notice a beautiful array of flowers all around me. I feel the sun on my back. And I'm happy. I've brought my skipping-rope with me and I start to skip. And I count out loud. One for each two jumps. I'm shouting the numbers and when I come to nine, I stop. It seems I can't skip any more. Every time, it's always nine. Then I wake up.'

I looked at him for some explanation. He was silent, watching me closely.

'The trouble is,' I went on, 'that I wake up in a sweat, and very afraid. What I don't understand,' I said, 'is that the dream is so beautiful, yet it turns out to be a nightmare.' Even as I spoke, I felt the sweat on my forehead, and my knees began to tingle.

'Does the number nine have any meaning for you?' Dr Fortescue asked.

It was the number of my crusade, I suddenly realised, and for me it had more than enough meaning.

'No,' I said. I was shouting. 'None at all.' I didn't want any probing. I didn't want any explanation. With a shattering clarity I now understood why my so-benign dream had turned into a sour nightmare. And it was none of Fortescue's business. I had to get out of there before my sweat betrayed me. I took the string out of my pocket.

'I've come to kill you,' I said. 'And may God forgive me.' It was the first time in my crusade that I had asked for forgiveness. I was getting soft, and with three more to go, I could not afford remorse.

He didn't seem in the least bit fazed by my threat.

'I understand,' he said. 'Now relax and breathe deeply. Take your time. Your dream is very strong,' he said, 'very interesting.'

'I'm going to kill you,' I said again.

His lack of fear infuriated me. 'I mean it,' I said. But the more I said 'I mean it', the less he was convinced.

'You're taking up my time,' he said.

'You're taking up *my* time,' I managed to say, and I heard my voice breaking like a growing schoolboy. I slipped behind him, and with my gloved hands I forced him into his chair and got on with the business. I checked his torpor and was satisfied.

I got out of there as quickly as I could. It had not been a pleasant dispatch. I recalled my euphoria after dear Mademoiselle Lacroix's *coup de grâce*. Dr Fortescue's killing had left a sour taste. It was not my touch that I was losing. It was my appetite. This worried me and I had to meticulously recap on every aspect of my motives. I had to image them again in the hope that they would nurture the need for my crusade.

There were some people around as I left Dr Fortescue's house and it's possible that I was seen. But I was not particularly noticed. A schoolboy was no oddity in that neighbourhood, and I walked with confidence to my car. I made sure that no one was about when I reached it. I got inside and drove a little way, then parked in a lay-by and quickly changed back into my regular clothes. I drove back to my office, poured a stiff whisky, and set myself to thinking.

Why am I writing this diary? Is it for myself or, as in some diarists' cases, is it written for others to read? As to the latter, I am certain: it is for nobody else's perusal. For if others should read it, they would pronounce me guilty. It is true that I have killed, and that I shall go on killing until my mission is fulfilled. But the mission itself is the quintessence of innocence. It is a truly honest protest and, in the long run, it will fulfil its purpose. A noble purpose, which is simply for the benefit of mankind. I say that with no arrogance, but with absolute certainty. I started it late, long after the event that occasioned it. When that happened, I was in such despair of my future that I grasped at the first hand that offered comfort. It belonged to one Emma Lewis, and I told her nothing at all. All I gave her was my despair. She didn't know the first thing about me. I valued myself so little, I couldn't imagine that anything about my person could be of interest. She tolerated two years of my silence, and then could bear it no longer. She was tired of dying in my company, and she left me to find some kind of life for herself. I didn't blame her. Fortunately we had no children.

At the time I was working as a junior partner in an accountant's office. I was not happy with my employers, and they in turn were not happy with me. I have to confess that, due to my sullen nature, I was almost unemployable. Moreover, I was lonely. I longed for companionship, but I was wary. I felt I had so little to give. I simply didn't want to be known. Then, by some miracle, I met Verry. Verry fitted the bill exactly. She accepted my silence and asked no questions. She seemed to be eternally grateful. In so far as I could love anyone at all, after the horrendous event that occasioned this diary, in so far as I could conceal my heart yet still love, that person was Verry. We were married, and shortly afterwards I came into a legacy and started up on my own. I managed to build up a regular clientele and make a comfortable living. By then we had two lovely boys, twins, Martin and Matthew. We have been together for many years now and if Verry is grateful, her gratitude cannot exceed mine. I consider myself blessed. Yet I still do not want to be wholly known. The event to which I referred has condemned me to a semi-life. It has stilled my tongue.

So perhaps I am writing this diary for myself alone. To put words on paper. Words which refuse to come out of my mouth. When I think of all the killings, I only half believe them, but once written down, detail by detail, they achieve some credibility. And they astonish me. These deeds are not in my nature. I was a gentle boy, gentle to the point of timidity. Yet these are *my* deeds, *my* killings. But the force that leads to them all is overpowering. And will not, in the name of love and loyalty, be denied.

To date I have killed six human beings. It is they who are guilty. I have to kill three more to complete my mission and then, whatever happens to me, I shall rest easy. The killings are a protest against evil. And, as God is my judge, I am innocent.

SIX DOWN. THREE TO GO.

When the news of the sixth killing landed on Wilkins' desk, it fell into the hands of his deputy. His boss was on holiday, somewhere in Scotland, and he debated with himself and other officers, whether Wilkins should be informed. Some were against interrupting their chief's holiday but most of them acknowledged that the shrink investigation was Wilkins' baby – always had been – and that he should be told immediately of the new development.

And, as they expected, Wilkins lost no time in coming back to work. He read all the facts of the case that were available. Dr Fortescue had been a well-respected psychotherapist. Among his duties was a weekly visit to the local public school to act as counsellor to those boys who needed guidance. Wilkins did not expect a break-in. Neither did he expect any kind of prints. But this case was different from the others. Although clearly by the same guitar-string garrotter, there were witnesses. Three of them to be precise. And all tallied in their testimony. One had seen a lad in uniform leaving Dr Fortescue's house. He looked like a sixth-former from the public school. He seemed to be in a hurry. The two other witnesses had seen what appeared to be the same boy walking in the street close to Dr Fortescue's house.

Wilkins was at first delighted, but he harboured doubts that a mere schoolboy could turn out to be such a vicious and cunning killer. Still, in all his investigations, it was the closest he had come to a clue.

He arranged an urgent meeting with the headmaster of the school, Dr Osborne, and presented himself in his office that very afternoon. He was invited into Dr Osborne's study and offered afternoon tea.

'It's about Dr Fortescue,' Wilkins began.

'A terrible business,' Dr Osborne said. 'A wonderful man, and so understanding of children. There's not a lot I can tell you about him personally. He tended to keep himself to himself. We talked together but only about the children, and I always took his advice.'

'We have some witnesses,' Wilkins said, coming straight to the point. 'And that's why I'm here. I'm afraid one of them saw a boy from the school – it could have been a sixth-former – leaving Dr Fortescue's house round about the time he was killed. Two other witnesses saw what appeared to be the same boy walking along a street near Dr Fortescue's house. Have you any idea what a pupil might be doing at Dr Fortescue's house at that hour?'

'It's preposterous.' Dr Osborne almost laughed. 'They must have been mistaken. If a student wanted to see Dr Fortescue, he would wait until his Thursday visit. He would have no need to make a personal call.'

'Nevertheless,' Wilkins insisted, 'I must take all sightings seriously. Out of courtesy, I have to ask your permission to interview all your sixth-formers. And separately, of course.'

'As you wish,' Dr Osborne said. 'I'm sure they'll enjoy it enormously. Any excuse to take them out of the classroom. But I have to tell you, Inspector, Dr Fortescue didn't counsel the sixth-form boys. He spent his Thursdays in the Junior School. With the boarders mostly. Homesickness. That sort of thing. I don't think the sixth-formers could shed any light on the crime.' He laughed again, and Wilkins rather hoped that in time, Dr Osborne would be laughing on the other side of his face.

'I'm obliged,' he said. 'Tomorrow morning. Nine o'clock. Is that suitable?'

'I will be expecting you,' Dr Osborne said.

Wilkins was hopeful. It was only a chink of light but one that, if well directed, could easily reach to the end of the tunnel. On his return to the station, he appointed his deputy to accompany him to the school. The deputy could not match Wilkins' optimism. He had his doubts, so together they made an able grilling pair.

The headboy, Hopkins, was the first to be interviewed. Witnesses had guessed the boy's height at about five foot ten, and of slim build. Hopkins was barely five and a half feet and round as a barrel. But out of courtesy, they questioned him as to his whereabouts at the time. Hopkins was a boarder, and at eight o'clock he was at breakfast along with a dozen others who could testify to his presence. This went for all the boarders at the school. There was only one sitting, at seven-thirty, and roll-call ratified their attendance. That left about twenty dayboys from the lower and upper sixth to be interviewed. The deputy's doubts seemed confirmed, but Wilkins still clung to his hopes. They went through them all and all offered the same breakfast alibi. They were at home, with their cornflakes. 'Mum or Dad'll tell you,' most of them said.

Harris was the last to arrive. He apologised for keeping them waiting. He had work to catch up with.

As Wilkins looked him over, he felt an involuntary thrill ripple through his whole body. Harris was five foot ten and of slim build.

'I suppose you're going to say you were at breakfast, like the others,' the deputy remarked without interest.

'As a matter of fact, I wasn't,' Harris said. 'I missed it. I had to do an errand for my father.'

'So exactly where were you at eight o'clock in the morning on Friday last?'

'I was with Dr Fortescue,' the boy replied. 'A bit before eight actually. Say a quarter-to.'

The thrill rippled still, but hiccuped around the base of Wilkins' spine.

'I must have been the last person to see him alive,' Harris said. He seemed proud of that fact.

The boy's honesty did not mark him out as a killer. But Wilkins pressed on. In his time, he had known boasting murderers, and Harris could well be one of them.

'What were you doing there?' he asked.

'Dr Fortescue is a close friend of my father. Or was, I suppose. My dad's a psychotherapist too, and he'd written a paper on adolescence that he wanted Dr Fortescue to comment on. I dropped it in on my way to school.'

The thrill fizzled out. This was the boy whom the witnesses had spotted. And that was the end of the matter. They were back to square one. No clues, no prints, no break-in. No useful witnesses after all.

'Thank you Harris,' Wilkins said. 'That will be all.'

He was tempted to add a warning to the boy about his father who was in the same perilous profession as the victim, but he did not want to alarm him. So it was back to the station to sift through the contents of Dr Fortescue's desk, and, unsurprisingly, they found Dr Harris's thesis on adolescence. It had been on top of the desk. It was open to page ten, and there were comments in the margins. It was on page ten that the killer had called.

During his absence, Mrs Wilkins had rung from the hotel in Scotland. He called her back. She wanted to know if he was returning to finish their holiday but he had lost all appetite for a break in his work. Although there was nothing more he could do in the Fortescue investigation, he wanted to stay put, even to be doing the nothing. The long-suffering Mrs Wilkins decided to stay on.

'Might as well,' she said. 'We've paid anyway.'

'I'll make it up to you,' Wilkins said, though he had no idea how or where. He was totally shrink-obsessed. Even when the killer took a break, he waited impatiently for a further strike. Practice did not necessarily make perfect, and the man was bound, eventually, to slip up.

There was much work to be done at the station. Robbery, muggings, even the occasional murder but none of these crimes stirred in him the slightest interest. He did what had to be done, and in routine fashion. He was biding his time.

He went to Dr Fortescue's funeral. He had been to the funerals of all the murder victims, and on each occasion, he had made notes. He fixed faces in his mind's eye. He hoped to find the stranger, one who was in no way related to the deceased; the stranger who would appear at every burial and whose repeated attendance would be question-able. But no such stranger appeared. For the most part the funerals were sparsely attended. Lonely people they had been, Wilkins surmised, their patients, however bereaved, unwilling to show their faces. Families mostly, if they had any, for all but one had lived alone. He had travelled to Barry Island for Bronwen Hughes' interment, and had stood by the graveside with only the local vicar for company.

It was almost as bleak in Birmingham, where Angela Mayling had been laid to rest. It was only in Paris that he had found a decent attendance, jollity even, and a right old rave-up wake afterwards. The gendarmerie wondered what he was doing there, for they considered Mademoiselle Lacroix their own business. But he had come to look for that same stranger who, he remained convinced, was responsible.

After the murder of Dr Fortescue, Dr Arbuthnot was again called in for his opinion. He stuck to his first diagnosis, and he had nothing further to offer. He confessed himself as bewildered as Wilkins himself. In desperation, and on the quiet, Wilkins called on a clairvoyant. She had hitherto been useful to the service in pinpointing the location of bodies. And sometimes she had been accurate.

But Wilkins knew very well where the bodies were. No attempt had been made to hide them. It was the whereabouts of the perpetrator he was after, and although he had as little faith in clairvoyance as he had in therapy he was a desperate man. And in desperation, all avenues must be exploited.

He had worked with Miss Lupesco before, and he looked forward to the glass of mulled wine she always served before her seances. Her parlour was unadorned, and she likewise. She wore a tweed skirt, a silk blouse and sensible shoes. Her hair verged on ginger, and neatly framed a slightly florid face. Wilkins suspected high blood-pressure or perhaps an over-indulgence in mulled wine. However, in all respects, she cut a conventional figure and, but for a crystal ball on a small table, she could have passed as a simple spinster, devoted to good works.

She offered him a glass, but refused one herself. Then

she sat opposite him at the table. She placed her hands around the crystal ball and closed her eyes.

'Tell me all you know,' she said.

So Wilkins started from the very beginning, with the first victim Harry Winston. And as he told his long and sorry tale, he felt an enormous relief, an unburdening as it were, and he warmed towards Miss Lupesco much as a patient, he thought, might warm to the therapist. When he was done, Miss Lupesco opened her eyes. Her fingers were light on the ball, and they quivered at times, as did her lips.

Wilkins waited. He was happy to enjoy his relief in the silence that followed. At last she spoke. 'I'm not sure it is a man,' she said.

Those were her first words and Wilkins was jolted. Had he been barking up the wrong tree all this time?

'I see a woman sometimes,' she said. 'And then there are men. Perhaps it is a man in disguise. Gloves seem to be important here. White gloves, or black. But they are always there. Prominently. There's a car. Red. Not a new one. Looks much travelled. I see twins. Boys. They are very important. But I don't see a connection. Yes. I think it is probably a man. He is crying. He is in great distress. There is a scream inside him. And a rope.'

Quickly she covered the ball with a black cloth. 'I can't go further,' she said. 'Perhaps next time.'

She seemed anxious for him to leave, disturbed by her sightings. And so was Wilkins, though he had doubts about clairvoyance. He recapped what she had told him, and it was the rope that stuck in his mind. And the scream. He couldn't fathom either, but he sensed that both were crucial. He was also aware of her doubts about gender. It had never occurred to him that the killer could be a woman. Neither had the possibility of disguise. That was a factor he must consider in future investigations – if there were to be any. And with shame, he half hoped that they would continue, for he was determined to get to the bottom of the shrink mystery. He began to look upon it as a crusade.

It is the boys' birthday. Twenty-six today. It's difficult to buy presents for people who have everything, but there's a shop in the West End that caters for this problem. It sells silly things. Useless and expensive. I bought them each a miniature model of a Porsche, one that dispensed soda water. They were cocktail people, my boys, and I thought it very suitable. I'd arranged my treat carefully. Since Donald's arrest – and I don't know why – I've become more of the 'Verry' he always called me. I find myself making decisions, organising things. Like this birthday treat. Apart from the presents, I had booked three seats at the National, for a performance of *King Lear*. I was careful in my choice. I thought it would do them no harm to view the break-down of a father at the hands of his ingrate children. Or at least two of them. But I only needed two. It would be something to talk about at supper in the small restaurant that I had booked. Yes, I had arranged it all very carefully. I think it will be a birthday treat that my boys will remember, but not necessarily enjoy. For I was determined not to condone their neglect as far as their father was concerned. Or worse, oblivion.

My boys were familiar with the play. They had studied it at university. And so was I, because I liked to be part of their studies. So we were all reasonably well equipped.

It was a wonderful production; the storm effects were breathtaking, and I could not fault the performers. Yet as we left the theatre, eavesdropping on rave reviews, the boys were subdued, and I was glad of it, for it meant that the message had struck home. It was a grand hors d'oeuvre in preparation for our supper.

It was a small restaurant and I'd ordered a corner table. There were few diners, and there was no music to drown what might have been our silence. The boys said nothing, so it was up to me to start the prickly ball rolling.

'What did you think of the acting?' I asked. Safe ground. I would come to the content of the play later.

'I thought Edgar was wonderful,' Martin said. 'And the Fool.'

Between them they praised or criticised most of the cast. But there was no mention of Lear and his daughters.

'What about the king?' I had to ask.

'If you think about it,' Matthew said, 'he asked for it. What he did was foolish.'

'Foolish yes. But not criminal,' Martin said.

They were both tired of pussyfooting.

'We're not going to see him,' Matthew said.

'And that's final,' Martin echoed.

I had played all my cards. No trumps. They had not even allowed for argument. Their decision was beyond debate. And it was final. But I would not surrender. 'I went to see him a couple of weeks ago,' I said. 'It was a lovely trip on the ferry.' I waited for them to at least ask how he was, how he was settling into a life sentence.

'What about a dessert?' Martin asked. 'I feel like a crème brûlée.'

It was like a slap in the face, Donald's as well as my own. But through the lump in my throat, I persisted. 'He's done some beautiful paintings,' I said. 'Seascapes. He recalls our Margate holidays together.'

No response. I sensed that in their silence, they were

beginning to pity me. 'He was a good father to you,' I added helplessly.

'Mum,' Martin said, with infinite patience.

I was grateful that at least he didn't address me as 'Mother'.

'Mum,' he said again. 'That was in another life. That was when he was another person. All that is in the past. It's history. It has nothing to do with us now.'

'Look,' Matthew interrupted. 'We respect how you feel. You must cope with it in your own way. Let us cope with it in ours.'

'I don't understand you,' was all that I could say. 'He always asks after you,' I added. I was lying. During my last visit, Donald hadn't mentioned the boys and it occurred to me that perhaps he also had consigned his sons to history, and that his, too, was altogether another life. In which case, it was only I who was holding the fort, who was keeping the home fires burning – but just for myself. I refused to differentiate between the past and the present. The former gives shape to the latter and I am undeniably part of both.

When the waiter passed by our table, I signalled for the bill. There had been enough of a treat, I thought, and crème brûlée wasn't going to be part of it. We waited in silence for the bill to arrive, and when it came I paid it hurriedly. I was anxious to get home. I wanted to be where I was unseen and unheard, some small corner where I could weep my heart out. The boys put their arms around me, and it was difficult not to howl aloud.

'Thank you,' Matthew said. 'It was a lovely birthday treat.'

'Can I at least give him your love?' I begged. My persistence, futile as it was, was getting on my own nerves. And, as I expected, they were silent. For to send their father their love would be an acknowledgement of his continued existence, and they had made it more than clear that he was dead for them.

They helped me into the car. Matthew drove, and Martin sat with me in the back. He kept his arm around me.

'I love you, Mum,' he whispered. 'So does Matthew. That will never change.'

I should have been satisfied. But it was a one-parent love they were offering, and to accept it spelt betrayal. So I said nothing, and nothing more all the way home.

Once inside, I shed all those tears that, in the restaurant, had been sent back to where they came from. I saw Donald in his prison gear and I was overwhelmed with a feeling I couldn't quite define. It could have been love for him, but possibly it was one of protection. Or perhaps they were one and the same.

THE DIARY

STILL SIX DOWN. THREE TO GO.

I prefer to think of it as two. Two to go. I was eager to make the last call of my mission. No preparations for that one. Above all, no gloves. But I had to put it out of my mind – till its proper time.

Dr Fortescue was a doddle. I read in the papers that there were witnesses. People had seen a public schoolboy. But it didn't worry me. That was all the information the newspapers divulged. Then they went pretty quiet, and I imagined the police had slipped up. Old Wilkins had probably interviewed the whole of the sixth form. Poor bugger. I must be driving him crazy.

So, a few weeks later, as much for his sake as mine, I decided to take a breather. To take Verry off for a weekend somewhere. Somewhere in the English countryside. Anywhere peaceful and quiet. Verry has been wonderful. She knows nothing of what I've been up to. And never will. There is no one I can tell. It's too painful. Far too painful. But in so far as a man of my nature and experience can love at all, I have loved Verry with all that is left of my heart. I've done my best by her. So I decided on a little English village. A shrinkless village, where I would not be tempted. Where I would live gloveless for a while, and bide my time.

We drove to a little Kentish hamlet where I'd heard of a small country house that welcomed weekend guests. Verry was so excited. That's what I love about her. She has not totally left her childhood behind. She whooped with joy at the sight of the four-poster bed, and I considered myself blessed. I felt safe with her. Safe from questioning. She is a monument to total acceptance.

I was glad to be out of London. To distance myself from the site of my pain was a measure of relief. But only a measure. Because my mind was never free of my crusade and the agony that had launched it. There are two Donald Dorrickses, one whom Verry and the boys know. But only I know the other Donald and I have to keep it a secret because it is untellable. I wonder sometimes whether the fulfilment of my mission will soften the pain, that when it is complete, the other Donald can freely be known, for it is too heavy a burden to carry alone.

I had to change my shirt before dinner. I persuaded Verry to go downstairs and wait for me at the bar. She agreed without any demur, which surprised me because Verry is shy by nature. But she is also obedient. I adjusted my tie and looked in the mirror, and I wondered which Donald I was seeing. Or rather which Donald the mirror reflected. For sometimes I confuse the two of them, and that is a dangerous jungle that might well unhinge me before my mission is accomplished.

Verry was waiting for me at the bar. She was talking animatedly to a woman, and I wondered what had happened to my shrinking violet of a wife. I think that the sight of the four-poster bed must have boosted her confidence. I approached them, and Verry made the introductions.

'This is my husband,' she said, and I put out my hand to the woman.

'Mary Wilkins,' she said. 'My husband will be along shortly. We're here for the weekend.'

As she was speaking, I noticed how my outstretched hand was trembling. It was the name that was melting my bowels. There are thousands of Wilkinses, I told myself, as I limply shook her hand, but the name was enough to unman me. I wanted to flee before her husband's arrival. I would know his face. It had appeared often enough in the newspapers and on television on my behalf. A bewildered face, frustrated, and with good reason. And then it presented itself at my side. And I trembled.

But not so much with fear as with a sudden exhilaration. And sense of power. For it was by my leave that the man was here in the first place. It was I who had given him a breather. I did not view it as a coincidence that, out of the thousands of English hotels, we had both chosen the same. It was not mere accident. It was fate. Chosen and planned. And I felt that I had engineered it all; that poor old Wilkins was my bait and that though I could use him to catch nothing, I could dangle him at my pleasure.

'Are you on holiday?' Verry was asking.

'Just a couple of days,' Wilkins said. 'Have to be back at work on Monday.'

I was tempted to tell him that there was no need. That there would be no devastating shrink-note waiting for him on his desk and that I would take my own time in causing one. I would make him itch for clues I would not leave, for witnesses who had seen nothing, for prints that were invisible. I would dangle him on my hook until I was ready to offer him a catchful of promise, but one that would get away like all the others.

And with these thoughts in mind, was it any wonder that I felt I had him in my power? I gave him my hand, the only print he'd ever get out of me.

'Pleased to meet you,' I said. I gripped his proffered paw.

He would not forget that handshake. Nor my name, which I donated loud and clear.

'Donald. Donald Dorricks,' I said. It was a name, then unknown, a name to be reckoned with at a future date, a date that I would determine. Then he would recall that handshake of mine, even feel it once more and his hand would tingle with rage and my name in his ear would thunder with fury.

I suggested we dine together. The enjoyment of power has no limits. Over the meal, we discussed our professions. I offered mine first. An accountant. It held no interest for anybody, least of all for myself. I wanted to get it over and done with because I was anxious to hear of Wilkins' profession, and to feign fascination in a calling of which I was already acutely aware. When he gave it across the table, Verry, bless her, was excited and it was she who introduced the murders and asked for Wilkins' prognosis.

He feigned an optimism in which he clearly had no confidence. 'We're on to him,' he said. 'It won't be long now.'

You're sitting right next to him, you silly bugger, I thought, and my sense of power was sublime. I could barely contain myself and, for my own relief, I changed the subject and asked them whether they had been to the Manor House before and what they knew of the county. It turned out that Mrs Wilkins was originally from these parts and this topic of conversation, though dull, lasted us through dinner. I have to confess to a measure of relief when the meal was over and especially when they announced that they would be leaving early in the morning to call on one of Mrs Wilkins' relatives who lived in the area. To add to my relief, no attempt was made to exchange addresses with the purpose of further meetings. That would have been a terrible risk, and a threat to that power of mine that was already perilously close to explosion. But its euphoria lingered for the remainder of the weekend and in its glow, I treated Verry with all the love of which

I am pathetically capable. I gave no thought to a further sortie of my mission. Delay would give me pleasure, for I could keep Wilkins waiting. Let him trumpet his empty optimism, nurture his futile hopes. His prognosis was at my dictation. His future was in my hands, and he could do nothing about it.

STILL SIX DOWN. THREE TO GO.

Wilkins' colleagues had urged him to take time off. They had noticed how the shrink murders were getting to him, eating away his usual confidence. He had listened to them, and gone to the Manor House for the weekend. But he couldn't relax. Every second of that weekend he was pricked with the urge to get back to work and he prayed for a note on his Monday-morning desk that would offer him another chance.

And there was indeed a note. But it irritated him.

'What have missing persons to do with me?' he asked his deputy. 'That's not my department. 'Give it to Brown. Let him deal with it.'

'It was Brown who passed it over to you,' the deputy said. 'He thought it might be of interest.'

Wilkins picked up the memo. '"Georgia Yonge,"' he read aloud. '"Reported missing, Saturday ten-thirty p.m. Not seen or heard from for six days." So?' Wilkins turned to his deputy. 'What's of interest to me?'

The deputy sniled. 'Everything, sir,' he said. 'The woman's a psychotherapist.'

Hope kindled once more. 'Any relatives?' Wilkins asked. 'A husband.'

'Let's go.' Wilkins was already reaching for his coat. 'Without doubt my department,' he said.

Mr Yonge himself opened the door. He wore that distraught look that Wilkins expected.

'May we come in?' the deputy asked, having shown his identity. They were invited inside.

'Have you found her?' Mr Yonge asked, fear in his voice.

'No,' Wilkins said. 'Not yet. We just wanted a word.'

They were not asked to sit down. Mr Yonge was a pacer and in the circumstances he felt no one else was entitled to relax. Wilkins asked the usual questions. Had there been a domestic quarrel? A crisis of any kind? Something special that would have worried her?

'No.' And emphatically, Mr Yonge added, 'Absolutely nothing!' He insisted they had a good marriage, protested rather, which seemed to give the lie to that statement. Wilkins was losing hope. This disappearance was a simple domestic and had nothing to do with his department. The woman would turn up, sooner or later.

And indeed she did. Washed up on the shoreline, some miles from home, and after a week in the water. It was then that witnesses came forward. A woman had been seen leaning over Battersea bridge. Another witness actually saw her jump. But from afar, and too distant to try to stop her. No, she hadn't reported it. Didn't want to get involved. Didn't think it was any of her business. 'If she wanted to make an end to life,' she shouted at Wilkins, 'I didn't see why I should interfere. And it's none of your business either,' she added.

So that was poor Mrs Yonge wrapped up, and her husband to be comforted. But apart from the comfort, there was the search for motive. And it was this aspect of the case that Wilkins sensed as a clue to the larger investigation.

He left the comfort to a woman officer, and after she had done her 'sorry' bit, he called on Mr Yonge to pump him for motive.

For some time, the man insisted on a happy marriage and he was at pains to provide proof and illustration. It was up to Wilkins to ask the leading question. 'Was your good wife in any way disturbed by the spate of killings of those in her profession?'

It was as if the widower had been waiting for such a question, unwilling to suggest such a connection himself. And then he came into his own, and there was nothing stopping him. 'Of course,' he said. 'She worried about it all the time. Ever since the whole terrible business started. She took every precaution, but I work in the City and she was alone most of the time. With each killing, she got more and more depressed. She knew Dr Fortescue very well. They were close friends. They met at conferences. And it wouldn't surprise me if it was his murder that tipped her balance. When are you going to catch him, Inspector?'

Then the man just fell into weeping and Wilkins suspected there was more to Mrs Yonge's friendship with Dr Fortescue, a friendship that went beyond the conference table. But all that was now irrelevant, except for the obvious and frightening threat of spin-off. A spin-off that might lead to further suicides and breakdowns, and a depressing pall of responsibility engulfed him. Another murder, he begged to himself. Just give me one more chance, and I'll crack it.

Although Mrs Yonge had not been a murder victim, Wilkins nevertheless went to her funeral, in the vain, yet eternal, hope that he would find the stranger. It was a small gathering, with few mourners. As far as he could ascertain, there were no patients present, which hardly surprised him. But there were no colleagues either. It was as if no one wished to be associated with the event, lest they be seen as suitable targets for the next elimination. Fear made for a barren burial, and Mr Yonge wept alone.

When Wilkins returned to his desk, he again recapped on the previous killings, and as before discovered no clues. What's more, the public was getting angry. The newspapers were full of letters of protest and indignation – all with addresses withheld. The Government was also disturbed and pressure was brought to bear on the Chief Constable who, with little hesitation, passed it on to Wilkins. At one point he even suggested that Wilkins take a short break. But Wilkins would have none of it. He would not let it go. He would get to the bottom of it. But how he would reach that bottom, he had absolutely no idea.

Visiting day. I was up early. I took great care with my dressing. I needed to look attractive. Not only for Donald's sake, but for my own. For I was lacking in confidence and unsure of my feelings, and although good dressing would affect neither, it would cloak my doubts in the eyes of the outside world. But that world did not include Mrs Cox, whom I had no wish to fool, for I knew that we were sisters under the skin. I looked forward to seeing her again. I would not mention the boys during my visit, and I relied on Donald to do likewise. I took him some extra brushes and paints but I had lost confidence in their association with Alcatraz and Hollywood. All that was cloud-cuckoo land and I realised that such dreaming was too insubstantial to tide me over Donald's prison term. I would have to find another way. I intended to spend the duration of the train journey to Portsmouth working out some alternative.

I arrived early at the station and the train was already standing at the platform. I found myself a comfortable window seat facing the engine. I like to see where I am going. I took out my notebook and a pen to jot down my thoughts, for I find that when I translate them into words I have to take them more seriously. To begin with, I wrote the heading: 'The boys' suggestions.' I wish I'd never thought of it, and certainly not as a first choice. So I was deeply relieved to see Mrs Cox making her way down the carriage. On seeing me, she smiled and settled herself on the seat opposite mine.

129

'Here we go again,' she said. 'And I don't know why. Sometimes I don't think he'd miss me if I didn't visit.'

'Of course he would,' I said, and I thought what a blessing it would be for us both, if our men were indifferent to our visits. Then we could simply stop going and no one could apportion blame. But I would miss my visits. They were the punctuation of my life. They measured my days, and without them, I would surely crumble.

I noticed that Mrs Cox was holding a carrier-bag. 'What have you brought him?' I asked.

'A couple of books he asked for. Gardening books. About roses. He's fixed on them. They let him tend the prison gardens from time to time.'

The word 'redemption' came to my mind. And I wondered whether he had been rose-fixated before he axed his wife's mother. And, as if she read my thoughts, Mrs Cox said, 'Roses have been his hobby since he was a boy. There's nothing he doesn't know about them.'

It didn't add up. Roses and murder, and I wondered how it added up for Mrs Cox.

'I'm going on holiday next month,' she said. 'I shall miss my next visit. And I'm afraid to tell him.'

'You're entitled to a holiday,' I said, and wondered whether I should take one myself. 'You can't serve his sentence to keep him company.'

'He'll go bananas,' she said.

And he did. In the visitors room, and in the hearing and sight of prisoners and visitors, the word 'Holiday?' he yelled. The offensive word shook the chairs and tables, which rocked into silence. Mr Cox was standing, his hands stretched towards his wife's neck, and had he not been quickly restrained, she would surely have joined her late lamented mother.

They took him away. His wife looked after him helplessly, then she made her own way out of the room, and I knew that soon I would find her crouched in the back of the bus, weeping her heart out.

The silence persisted. What had happened was a private matter and invited no comment, and it would have seemed insensitive to continue conversation that had been so rudely interrupted. But I took advantage of the event and I told Donald that all the woman wanted was a holiday and that was not such a terrible idea. And it only meant missing one visit. I was testing him, for I had in mind a holiday of my own. Then I thought that as far as Mr Cox was concerned, it was not the missed visit that vexed him. It was the thought of his wife having fun that caused his distress. That she could actually go off and enjoy herself when any kind of enjoyment was denied him. I wondered whether Donald would suffer the same resentment.

'Why shouldn't she take a holiday?' Donald obliged. 'You should take one too. Go up to Scotland. Stay with Frieda.' Frieda is my cousin. *She*'s got a manageable name. Pronounceable. But we're not very close. I think I'm jealous of her. Especially since Donald's episode. She's married and cosy, with two kids who live happily at home. I wouldn't visit Frieda. I couldn't bear her smugness. No. I'd go off on my own somewhere. A little hotel. By the Lakes perhaps. Or preferably somewhere hot. I'd stand at the bar. I'd had a rehearsal at the Manor House and that had led to good companionship. It could happen again. Someone would talk to me. I could be anybody, a hairdresser, a dress-designer, or even, God forgive me, a widow. The last thing I needed to be was a lag's left-over.

I became quite excited. 'I might do that, Donald,' I said. 'But between visits. I wouldn't want to miss one.'

He smiled at me. 'You're a good girl, Verry,' he said, and then I loved him all over again, and I knew that as long as I lived I would never desert him. And perhaps during my holiday, I could put pity aside.

He showed me his recent paintings. Seascapes again. One featured a lighthouse, another a clutch of fishing boats. I noticed that none of his paintings included people. But then he drew out a small sketch from the bottom of the pile.

'This is the latest,' he said, and with a little pride. It was a self-portrait. He was barefoot, with trousers rolled up, and his back was framed in a tranquil sea. It was Donald's dream of freedom. It was this picture he saw in the small sad hours of his waking, and as the darkness enveloped his cell. It was an image that gave him hope, that when and if he were ever free, the sea would still be there and would welcome his ageing trouser-rolled paddle. I leaned over the table and I kissed him. 'When you come out, we'll go to the sea again,' I told him.

The bell that marked the end of the visiting hour was well-timed. I was leaving with a conscience miraculously cleared of doubts, and I would hurry back to the bus and comfort Mrs Cox.

And, as I expected, there she was, crouched on the back seat of the bus, her head in her hands. I put my arm around her. I thought that gesture would be better than words. In any case, I had none to offer her. She let herself cry, and thus we travelled to the ferry. 'We'll go on deck,' I said. 'Get some fresh air.' I took her arm and guided her up the stairs. It was cold out there, but refreshing. We sat close to each other. And shivered. And I was glad of it because the cold was something positive to be concerned about. We withstood the nipping air for about ten minutes and then she made a move to go downstairs where there was warmth and a positive comfort. She cheered up a little as she settled herself into a window seat and I went to the bar and bought us a whisky each. By the time we reached Portsmouth, she was herself again.

'I'm going to take that holiday,' she said. 'Whatever he thinks.'

They were the first words she had spoken since we had left the prison.

'Where will you go?' I said.

'I've got a friend in Florida. A close friend. She was good to me during the trial. Came over especially to support me. She wants me to stay with her for a while. It's too far to go just for a fortnight. And too expensive. So I'll stay as long as she'll have me, and bugger Mr Cox.'

'You can put it all behind you for a while,' I said, 'and when you come back, you'll have the strength to carry on.'

'*If* I come back,' she said. And smiled.

But I knew she would come back. And in time for her visit. Indeed I wondered whether she would go away at all.

We parted at Waterloo, wishing each other well, and I returned home and started to make preparations for my holiday. The next day, I visited the nearest travel agent and brought home a collection of holiday brochures. I was looking for sun, a beach, music and a bar. My needs could have been satisfied by almost any one of the holidays on offer. So I picked out one brochure and opened a page at random. It fell on a ten-day break in a resort on the south coast of Turkey. I returned forthwith to the travel agent and booked a package holiday to the resort that left a couple of days later. I could return in good time for my prison visit. On my way home I kept saying 'Verry' to myself, pleased with the unfamiliar assertiveness that that name implied. I've grown into my name at last, I thought. I'll never let it trouble me again.

I had a good summer wardrobe, so preparations for travel took little time. I hesitated about informing the boys of my plans. They might interpret them as a change of heart, which they certainly were not. On the contrary, they were a confirmation of what my heart still held. Uncertainty and pity. But above all, love. I decided I would simply send them a postcard from my Turkish hotel.

I was glad that I was able to organise a holiday so quickly. Barely three days after my prison visit. It allowed me no time for hesitation or change of mind. I would be settled by the Turkish seaside before I could entertain second thoughts. And then it would be too late.

I was excited and almost ashamed of my excitement. I gave a thought to Mrs Cox and wondered how far she was on her way to Florida. I had a vision of her sitting alone in her house, thinking about her mother. But I banished such a thought. I was going to enjoy myself, to see for once to my own welfare, to 'Verry' myself, and to find it natural.

I had never been on an aeroplane before, and the fear heightened my excitement. I would pretend that I was a seasoned traveller and still the butterflies inside me. I decided that for the duration of the flight, I would be a hairdresser, a career that did not necessarily involve a great deal of specialised knowledge, and, if called for, I could divert the conversation to tales of my clients. But such a plan was scotched when my neighbour on the plane, a very friendly and direct type, introduced himself by name and profession. Mark Digby, he was, and a hair-stylist and he was very pleased to meet me. I had quickly to fashion a new career for myself. The idea of a kennelmaid flashed through my mind. I knew a little about dogs and their care, having owned a Scotch terrier as a child. But, as it turned out, I was not called upon to announce a pursuit of any kind, nor even my name, which I could have pronounced with no hesitation. My companion spent the whole four-hour flight talking about himself, with just one break for a short nap after lunch, for which I was very grateful. In any case, I wasn't too keen on the kennelmaid idea and I decided to use it only as a very last resort. Nevertheless, I was still in high spirits when we landed and I realised that, since leaving home, I hadn't given Donald a thought. This worried me a little, and made me wonder about the present fragility of our partnership. Then pity intervened and confirmed that it was indestructible. However, for ten days, I would try to put him out of my mind.

My spirits rose when we reached the hotel. My room sported a balcony that overlooked the sea, a blue-green sea, unlike the Margate variety and the colours of Donald's recall. There were still two hours to go before dinner, so I rested a little, then showered and dressed. As I took myself down to the bar, I felt very 'Verry' and faintly brazen.

Our courier was already ensconced at the counter, and he offered me the free welcome drink that the brochure had promised. Others of our party – we were about twenty in all – were gathered around the bar and seemed to be keeping themselves to themselves. Most of them gave the appearance of being in couples, glued to each other's side in silence. But there were a handful of lone travellers shifting uncertainly from one foot to the other. I found that I was doing the same, like a visual advertisement for singleness. Someone had to make a move, and it was little me, the non-Verry of old, who went over to a single woman to halt her shifting.

Her name was Penny, and she admitted to being nervous. 'It's the first holiday I've taken on my own,' she said. And then, as if to explain herself, she added that she had been recently widowed. I gave her my sympathies, though these seemed not to be required. He'd been ill for a long time, she was saying. It was a blessing when he went. I refrained from celebrating her blessing and I said, 'Yet you must miss him.'

She nodded. 'But life goes on.'

I thought the same for myself.

'And what about you?' she asked.

'Oh I'm married,' I protested. 'Just having a break. He's away, anyway. He's a portrait painter and he's been commissioned to do a portrait of the Queen of Jordan.' And I'm the Queen of Sheba, I thought to myself. Yet I was pleased with my invention. It kept Donald the painter by my side. Moreover, I didn't have to be anything in my own right. It was enough to be the helpmeet of a successful artist and I could spend my holiday promoting Donald the painter.

Penny was clearly impressed. I hoped I hadn't gone too far. It was a story I would have to maintain the length of my holiday and to all those of the party who sought to enquire. I prayed that there was no portrait painter among them.

In a short while, we were invited to take our places for dinner. Penny waited for me to move in order to follow me and no doubt to sit by my side. There were five tables reserved for our party. The couples walked boldly to their seats. The singles lagged behind, so that they ended up seated at the same table and although we were together, our unity seemed to heighten our otherness from the main party. Penny seemed glued to my side. Next to me sat a gentleman who introduced himself to me as Carruthers. 'Call me Jim,' he added.

'I'm Verry.' He'd have to do without my surname.

He took my hand. 'I'm glad to make your acquaintance.'

I was unused to such formality and especially when he picked up my napkin and spread it over my lap. This man will take care of me, I thought, and I shall allow it without any scruple.

I am reasonably familiar with Turkish food. Donald and I would often visit a Turkish restaurant. It is an intimate cuisine, unsuitable for sharing with strangers. Yet I was happy to share it with my neighbour.

'I always come to Turkey for my holidays,' he said. 'I just love the food.'

I asked him what he did, safe in the knowledge that my own response, if called for, was ripe and ready.

'I'm retired,' he said. 'From the army. I'm doing an Open University course in botany. Must keep the old cells active. And you?'

I pulled out my Donald portfolio and recounted the tale that had so impressed Penny.

'You're obviously very proud of him,' Jim said.

I nodded. Though I was anything but proud. You cannot sustain pride in a myth, and already it was losing its credibility. The reality was so different and called for nothing but humiliation. I was ashamed of Donald. Deeply ashamed. Innocent or guilty, there was no denying his location, and it was a far cry from the palaces of Jordan. But I was stuck with the story, and I hoped I wouldn't be called upon to spin it again, lest my own qualms betray me.

It was while Jim was helping me to wine that I felt his leg pressing on my own. I hoped my astonishment did not show on my face, or indeed my pleasure. For pleasure it was, I must confess, and I made no move to discourage him. Verry Dorricks, I said to myself, what are you doing here, away from the prison gates, on your own, with a stranger's leg pressing against yours, and all with your pleasurable permission. I couldn't understand myself. Never in all my years with Donald had I experienced an illicit thrill nor, more importantly, had I made myself available to one. I already saw myself as an adulteress, but I had no sense of betrayal. I'm forty-seven years old, I told myself, and I'm still entitled to happiness. I knew it was a dangerous thought and God knew where it would lead but I would follow it with pleasure.

The meal was over. It was late and I was tired, not so much as the result of the long journey, but because of the unaccustomed but wondrous battering of my senses. I made to rise. Jim was already standing. He held the back of my seat so that I could rise in comfort. I was feverish with his chivalry.

'A little nightcap?' he suggested, and he took my arm and led me towards the bar. As we walked, I noticed that he was limping.

'Have you hurt your foot?' I asked. That question signalled the dissolving of my euphoria.

'No,' he said. 'War wound. I've got a wooden leg.'

I checked that it was the very leg that had rubbed against mine. I tried to hide my shame. I had misread. I had misunderstood. Misconstrued.

'I'm tired,' I said. 'I think I'll just go to bed.'

I had to be alone. I had to unravel myself. The fact that the lecherous leg was wooden, unfeeling and without intent, that fact was irrelevant. It was *my* leg that starred in the role, my yielding and inviting leg that was clearly asking for more. By the time I reached my bedroom, I was crumbling with shame. I could have done without knowing that aspect of myself, and its discovery frightened me, for it pointed to what I was capable of, and to the inevitable break-up of my marriage. I thought of Donald sleeping in his cell, and I couldn't bear the pity and the love of it. I wanted very much to go home. But I had another nine days of the fabled palaces of Jordan and myself as a woman of virtue, worthy of praise. But I weathered it, and tried to enjoy myself. As the days passed, I gradually withdrew into my old Verry, or rather non-Verry, self. That assertiveness of mine was a mere passing phase. And a dangerous one, for it opened up avenues of excitement of which I had been unaware. I must not risk such a phase again. I must keep within those boundaries that I had fashioned for myself, and which my Donald had confirmed. I felt safe within them. Donald was innocent, because he said so, and he had never lied to me. He would be on his best behaviour in prison and he would earn an early parole. Then we would spend our days at the sea together and I wouldn't have to pity him any more. These were not cloud-cuckoo thoughts. They were within the realms of possibility.

On the last day of my holiday, I took a walk along the shore. Fallen stone pillars were strewn at intervals along the sand: torsos; broken stone heads; remains of temples where people had once worshipped; monuments to the glory of the past. All that was gone, and in its stead, a marketplace of carpets, saffron and sponges. I picked my way through Turkey's broken history and I decided that I was not a holiday person. I belonged at home, non-Verry within its walls. I would take my non-Verry self to Parkhurst, and comfortably believe in Donald's innocence.

THE DIARY

SEVEN DOWN. TWO TO GO.

I can't seem to get going again. I want to hold on to the power, that power I felt at the Manor House. I don't want to let it go. I want to keep Wilkins waiting. I want to see him pacing his room, itching for my next sortie. I want to hear him curse me aloud, unable to give a name to his target. I want him at my mercy for a little longer. But why? Wilkins is not my enemy. He has done me no harm. Why should I want to punish him? This is an ill trait in me and I must put it aside, for it sullies my crusade. In any case, in clinging to this sense of power, I might well lose my appetite for my mission, and that in the long run is far more important to me than Wilkins-baiting. Besides, it's quite a while since I polished off Dr Fortescue.

I read about that suicide. Dr Yonge. She was a friend of Dr Fortescue. But her suicide was none of my doing. So I won't chalk her up. Nevertheless, she was one of them. And now she is no more, and I didn't have to lift a finger. God is on my side after all.

I have to look around for another victim. That will leave only two. I am well on my way to vindication.

It was a woman's turn. I like to be fair in my choices, and I lit upon a Melissa Fairbanks who plied her dubious trade somewhere in Hertfordshire. I didn't need to use the Devon ploy. I could be there and back well within the day. I staked out the address and particulars before making my move. Melissa was a divorcee who lived alone. Her dwelling was a cottage that was generously isolated. She gave me an appointment at five o'clock in the afternoon. A poetic time I thought, for it is at this hour that the doomed bull enters the ring. There was a mini-market car-park near her home. It was pretty full, and I slipped into a space unnoticed. Then I walked across two fields to her cottage. I was gloved, of course, but that was the extent of my cover. I looked at my watch. It was exactly five o'clock and I almost heard the flourish of trumpets as the bull roared into the ring. I saw myself in my suit of lights, amply prepared.

I rang the bell and she opened the door herself.

'Mr Crawford?' she asked, for that was my seven-down two-to-go name.

'No,' I said. I had to. I couldn't perform. Wilkins would have to wait, for Miss Fairbanks was the spitting image of my Verry. The same colouring, the same hair, the same plump figure, the same smile.

'I'm sorry to disturb you,' I said quickly. 'I must have the wrong address. I'm looking for a Mr Thomas.' I was pleased with my prompt invention.

'I don't know a Mr Thomas in these parts,' she said. 'But you could ask at the post office in the village.'

'Thank you,' I said. 'I'm sorry to have troubled you.' I left her, crossing the fields without fear of witness, while Melissa waited for a Mr Crawford who had changed his mind. It was surely her lucky day. I was relieved for her, as I was for myself. I can't honestly say that I enjoy my sorties. I am killing after all, and that calls for little pleasure. Of course, I am thrilled each time I get away with it but that thrill is temporary and I have continually to bear in mind the purpose of my crusade. It is that which propels me. I thought of Verry. Her resemblance to Melissa had shaken me, and I valued her more and more. I thought I'd buy her a little treat, so I dropped into the mini-market with my trolley, like any respectable shopper, and I bought a side of smoked salmon and a good bottle of Chablis.

I had saved Wilkins a journey to Hertfordshire, and I wondered where he would like me to send him next. He'd already been to South Wales on my behalf, the London suburbs, Birmingham and, to top it all, Paris. I thought another journey to Kent might please him. He could take his wife along and she could visit her relations, while he was looking for clues and witnesses – of which there would be none. So I decided on Canterbury.

On investigation, I found the place riddled with psychotherapists. Perhaps it was the awesome aura of the cathedral and its pious overtones. Therapy must have been seen as a safe haven from its guilt-inducing severity. There was a Mrs Sheila Stephens practising there, audaciously in the precincts of the cathedral itself. Her location plainly proclaimed that she was offering an alternative. I was aware that it was a strike that entailed some risk – and a very special disguise. Mrs Stephens lived in a well-populated quarter, where tourists outnumbered residents. I first thought I might dress as one of them, an American perhaps, with a garish T-shirt and cigar. But that was too easy, too obvious and lacking in imagination.

A better disguise was that of a clergyman. In my reconnaissance I had noted that many men of the cloth ambled in the cathedral precinct. I made a note of their garb and their gait and I felt that both suited me. I hired the costume from a theatrical costumier. I told them it was for amateur dramatics, which was partly true. Drama it certainly was, but by now I was far from amateur. I didn't bother to make an appointment. The arrival of a clergyman at a Canterbury door would be no surprise. I would carry a box with me as though collecting for charity.

The cathedral clock struck four as I passed her doorway. I knew that sessions usually lasted about fifty minutes, and just in case she had a patient I would wait around until he or she left. But within ten minutes, a man emerged, looking rather distraught, I thought. His had clearly been a depressing session. I waited a while, then I boldly went to her door and rang her bell.

She answered almost immediately and smiled when she saw me. Men of the cloth are used to welcome and I returned her smile. I decided that this was going to be a quick one.

'I'm collecting for children in Ethiopia,' I said, and I stuck my foot in the door.

'Just a moment,' she said. 'I'm on the phone.'

I went straight inside.

'I'll be there at six,' I heard her say.

I wouldn't count on it, I thought. Then she came back. My string was at the ready. I took her from behind, rather as I had poor Miss Mayling about five killings ago. It was all over quickly. There was a lot of blood, but I kept myself spotless. I made sure her pulse was still, then I left, rattling my collection box, first making sure that no one was in the close. I joined a group of clergymen who were making their way to the cathedral. I acknowledged one of them and commented on the weather. But he shook his head. 'Spanish,' he said and I was relieved.

I had never been inside the cathedral and I thought I might as well do a bit of sightseeing. But once inside, I felt deeply out of place, and for good reason, and slowly I backed my way outside. I was anxious to get out of my disguise. I thought that without it my shame would cool. But it took some time, and I had reached the outskirts of London before I was calm again. The thought of the purpose of my mission justified all.

The following morning, I returned the costume to the costumier. The assistant asked me if the play was a success.

'Did you have a good house?' he asked.

'Full,' I said. 'Relatives.' I laughed.

'What was the play called?'

He'd caught me on the hop.

'*The Vicar's Lapse*,' I said off the top of my head.

'Sounds interesting,' he said.

I fled before he could question me further. I was glad to get rid of that costume and I resolved never to use such a disguise again. It was a temptation to fate. It was an insult, an offence, a base irreverence, and to whom I dared not contemplate. So it's

SEVEN DOWN. TWO TO GO.

It was Save the Children Week in Canterbury. Much work had gone into its promotion. Sundry committees had organised events which were to culminate in a grand fête in the city square. Coordinating all these committees was Mrs Sheila Stephens, a bigwig in the Canterbury community, a JP who sat on the Bench, and who, apart from all her good works, practised as a part-time psychotherapist. A final meeting of all the committees to coordinate events was scheduled to take place on a Thursday evening at six o'clock.

They were gathered in the council chamber of the Town Hall. The chairmen of each committee had prepared their progress reports. They were ready to begin. But they were missing their president. Mrs Stephens was a stickler for punctuality and they couldn't understand why she was late. Some emergency might have occurred, one suggested. She may be ill, said another.

'She's not ill,' a woman said. 'I spoke to her on the phone at about four o'clock. She said she'd be here at six.'

'Let's give her another ten minutes,' they decided. 'She's bound to have some explanation.'

Since it was Mrs Stephens' duty to authorise all the arrangements, it was impossible to proceed without her. The minutes went by. The gathering was restless and a little concerned. At six-thirty, the Reverend Tom Fenby, who was in charge of the tombola, offered to go round to the precinct and knock on her door. They all agreed and said that they would wait for his return.

When he was gone, they speculated on the causes of Mrs Stephens' absence.

'Cold feet at the last minute,' Mrs Havering suggested. She had never liked Mrs Stephens. Thought her a bossy-boots.

'I must say,' Mrs Gordon of the cake stall offered, 'it's quite a relief to be without her. She should never have been elected in the first place.'

'Amen to that,' Mr Naughton offered. He'd wanted to take charge of the coconut shy, but Mrs Stephens had ordered him to the ticket booth where he would be stuck for the whole afternoon and could enjoy nothing.

By the time the Reverend Tom Fenby returned, Mrs Stephens' reputation was in tatters. Unmendable, torn asunder by many bitter words, which later would have cause to be eaten and swallowed in shame. Or pretend that none of them had been said or heard.

They were appalled at Reverend Fenby's appearance. He was white. He struggled into the hall and groped for a seat. He was breathless with horror.

'What's the matter, for God's sake?' Mr Naughton asked. He waited for the Reverend to catch his breath

'Murder,' the Reverend panted. 'I called the police. I must get back there.' Then he put his head in his hands. 'God have mercy,' he said.

The committee men and ladies gathered around him. An event threatened, a real event, one far more exciting than cake stalls and tombolas.

'What happened?' one of them asked.

By now the Reverend Fenby had regained his composure.

'I knocked at her door. I rang her bell. I tapped on the window and there was no reply. Then I noticed a red streak that started under the front door and continued down the path. It looked like blood. I panicked. I broke the glass window of the front door and looked inside. She was lying face-up on the floor.'

His composure deserted him once more and he broke down, weeping.

The committee ladies had begun to put on their coats. They were bound for the scene of the crime.

'Poor Mrs Stephens,' Mrs Gordon said. 'Such a good woman.' She had clearly forgotten her expressed relief at being without her, and a murmur of fulsome praise was heard from the gathering. They helped Reverend Fenby to his feet, and together they made their way to the precinct.

The police were already on the spot, and the cul-de-sac where Mrs Stephens had lived was cordoned off. Two policemen stood guard outside the house, while a few in authority were allowed inside. Reverend Fenby approached one who looked like a senior officer, and confessed to having discovered the body and made the phone call. He was taken aside. By this time a sizeable crowd had gathered, and the police urged them to go away.

'Show's over,' they said, but the crowd would not move. And there they stayed until the nine o'clock bell tolled from the cathedral.

The investigators were still inside the house. Their search had ceased, but they were embroiled in argument. The Chief Superintendent reminded them that the murder was the business of Detective Inspector Wilkins. But the Chief Inspector considered it was his baby since the crime had been committed on his patch. So they argued, back and forth. It was a question of whether or not they should move the body. The Chief Superintendent argued that all should remain as it was found until Wilkins could see for himself. Eventually the Chief Inspector surrendered and a call was put through to London.

Wilkins had settled down to watch the news on television. His wife had brought him his cocoa, and suggested he have an early night. Then the telephone rang.

'Leave it,' Mrs Wilkins said. 'We could be out. Nothing's that important it can't wait till morning.'

'You never know,' Wilkins said, as he stretched his arm to the receiver.

His wife watched his face as he listened to the caller. Whatever it was, it must have been good news, for his eyes crinkled with joy.

'Tell them not to touch anything. And send the car. I'm ready to leave.'

He put the phone down. 'He's done it again,' he said. 'In Canterbury. At last another chance.'

'What about the poor victim?' Mrs Wilkins reminded him.

But he was already reaching for his coat. 'If killers are on the loose, there are going to be victims,' he said. He went over to her and put his arm around her shoulders. 'It's a nasty business,' he said. 'But you know that. It's part of the deal.'

'I'll get you a thermos,' she said. 'And a sandwich. You'll be up all night.'

Wilkins was not a religious man, but on the journey to Canterbury, he prayed. He prayed for a fingerprint, a stray fibre, a shoe print. He prayed for a witness. Just one reliable witness. He prayed for a clue of any kind. He had high hopes and he tried to stifle them. He had always had high hopes prior to each investigation, and each time they had come to naught. Sitting in the passenger seat, he drove with the driver, pressing his foot on the floor of the car. Accelerating. He was anxious to arrive.

The roads through south London were heavy with traffic but the siren facilitated their passage and the M2 to the coast was reasonably traffic-free. In just over an hour, they arrived in Canterbury. And straight into the close.

As soon as he saw the body, he recalled that of the second murder, Angela Mayling of Birmingham. Both women had been found in the same position. Taken from behind, face upwards on the hall floor. His hopes began to fade. The Birmingham murder had offered no clues at all and this one was likely to be the same. Apart from the glass pane which Reverend Fenby had broken, there was no sign of a break-in, the Chief Inspector informed him, no fingerprints, no shoes, no fibres. He insisted that their search had been thorough.

Wilkins felt *de trop*, and he began to wonder why he had been called upon.

'We thought you ought to see the scene as we found it,' the Chief Superintendent added.

'Has the pathologist been?' Wilkins asked.

'Yes. He put the death at between four and six o'clock. The cause is as you see.'

'Any witnesses?' Wilkins asked.

'We've covered that too.' The Chief Inspector was smug. Nobody saw anyone. Except a clergyman who was collecting for Save the Children Week. But they're all over the town this time of the year.

'Where was this clergyman?' Wilkins was desperate. 'Was he seen in the close?'

'No,' the Chief Inspector said. 'He was near by and he

was seen to join a group of them going into the cathedral. You surely don't think a man of the cloth—'

'It could have been a disguise,' Wilkins said. He recalled his session with Miss Lupesco. It was she who had suggested disguises. And what more obvious disguise for a Canterbury murder than the garb of a man of the cloth? But even if it was not a disguise, there was hardly any point in grilling the hundreds of genuine ministers who lived in and visited Canterbury. Especially in this tourist week. It was a dead end once more.

'Remove the body,' he said to the Chief Inspector. 'And thanks for calling me in. I'm afraid there's little I can do from London. Further investigations must be conducted from here. Your patch, Chief Inspector,' he said. 'Of course we will liaise on any further developments.' But Wilkins knew that there would be no further developments any more than there had been in the six previous cases. Not one of them had offered a single clue.

On the journey back to London, he asked his driver to take it slowly. He was in no hurry to get home. He needed to think about his position and to wonder whether he should offer his resignation to pre-empt the suggestion that he might be taken off the case. Or rather the cases. Seven of them, as it now was. And he had come up with nothing. Such a dismal record cried out for a demotion if not outright dismissal. Yet he was loath to leave. It would be a blatant admission of failure. The shrink cases were his baby. His obsession almost, and though he had gathered no solid evidence, he doubted that anyone else could do better. He decided to have a word with his superior. Somehow he had to acknowledge his failure, yet cling with certainty to a none-too-distant future solution.

This he did and his superior seemed to understand. And he would hear nothing about talk of resignation.

'You can't leave now, Wilkins,' he said, slapping him on the back. 'I'm depending on you.'

Wilkins wasn't sure whether he was flattered by his trust, or burdened with a dire responsibility.

I'm still ashamed. I can't put that wooden leg out of my mind. And how can I face Donald? He's bound to ask me about the holiday. I could tell him about most of it. Even about Jim. Even about his wooden leg. I didn't have to tell him about my own excited one. But when I thought about that holiday, that is, when I had the courage to think about it, it was my leg that coloured every recall. Even the saffron and the sponges in the marketplace were stained by it. Even the fallen pillars and the torsos on the sand had to suffer my leg's rude interference. Once, while remembering, I caught my face in the mirror and it was red with shame. So how could I face Donald with all that recall. It even crossed my mind to make some excuse and cancel my visit, to give time for my blushes to fade and the leg memory to wither. But I had no hope of that. I knew that I could never expunge that humiliation. But I had no right to deprive him of a visit. Somehow I had to weather it all.

I didn't even have a meeting with Mrs Cox to look forward to. She was probably still in Florida, and her axe-man spouse would be gnashing his teeth in his cell.

I dressed carefully. I was not sorry that my tan had faded, and it crossed my mind to deny that I'd been on holiday at all. I decided that that was a solution of sorts and I'd just have to go on making up events about life at home. I'd bought him a present in the market. A real sponge. But now I took that out of my bag, knowing that it would take more than a genuine sponge to wipe those memories clean. 'No, I decided not to go away, Donald,' I rehearsed en route to the station. 'Didn't feel like a holiday on my own.' That might please him, I thought. It was much easier to be a liar than a potential nymphomaniac. Because that's how I saw myself. I was hungry, and that hunger might well lead to other leg movements of mine. And, guilty or innocent, Donald would never again be by my side.

I wondered about my future. I had always tried to avoid such thoughts, for my prospects were bleak. I knew I had to do something. I had to stick with Donald, or leave him. But to do either, I had to be convinced of his guilt or innocence. But I had no evidence for either. I knew so little about him. By virtue of our many happy years together, he was innocent, but I could not ignore the verdict of the jury. Somehow I had to find evidence that pointed either way. I would have to find the courage to question him. I would not beat about the bush. I would say to him, 'Donald, did you really kill all those people?' And his answer would be, 'Yes. But I am innocent.' Exactly as he had answered from the dock. I didn't understand it then, and I don't understand it now. But I have to learn to understand it before I can stay with him. Or, God forbid, leave him to cope on his own. I found myself shivering at such a thought, and I hurried down the platform where the train was waiting.

I made my way to a window seat, and there she sat, as if waiting for me. Poor Mrs Cox, severely untanned, and Florida a ragged figment of her imagination. She looked ashamed.

'I didn't go away,' she said, as I took my seat opposite her. 'Didn't have the courage.'

'Neither did I,' I said. 'Same reason.' I was glad to have a rehearsal run for my lies and I was glad, too, to see her at all. But not all that surprised. I suspected that she would have had second thoughts. I warmed towards her. She was as tied to her axeman as I to my killer, and neither of us knew why. Both of us claimed loyalty and love and, above all, pity. But neither of us had sufficient self-esteem to turn away.

'I haven't brought him anything,' she said. She announced it as a triumph. 'Not after last time. He doesn't deserve anything. I don't know why I come at all.'

There was nothing I could say to that, so there was silence between us. Then, after a while, as the train started to move, she looked directly at me and said, 'Why do you come? Tell me.'

'For the same reasons as you,' I replied, 'and, like you, I don't know what they are.'

'I think this is my last visit,' she said.

But I knew that she didn't mean it. Compulsion would put her on that train and drive her over the ferry, urge her to sit across from that man she loved and loathed. And that same compulsion would force her into the decision never to visit again. Until the next time. Both of us were serving a life sentence.

Donald looks better each time I see him. He's filled out a little and he has a good colour. I checked the thought that prison was good for him. He was there at the table, waiting for me to arrive. I noticed that the axeman was waiting too. And his presence made me angry. How dare he so coldly assume that his wife would visit him? And already he had a look of victory in his eye. I had a mind to persuade Mrs Cox to write him off. But I would miss her company on the train and the ferry, someone with whom I could share my dilemma.

Donald rose when he saw me, and stretched out his arms.

I thought of the wooden leg and I went willingly towards him and kissed him heartily. It was the only way I could ask for his forgiveness.

'You're looking well,' he said. 'Did you go to Frieda's?'

'No,' I said, glad to be able to tell the truth. 'I didn't feel like going away.' I waited for him to declare his usual innocence. But it was not forthcoming. That puzzled me, and I wondered whether he was saving it until I had to leave.

'What's new?' he said.

'Nothing much. I keep busy.'

'With what?'

'The usual things. I've joined a dressmaking class,' I invented. 'I quite enjoy it.'

'You were always a great darner,' he said. 'Do you remember the days when I used to wear woollen socks?'

He was right. I loved darning. It made so much sense. All that weaving in and out. There's no call for that skill any more. Nylon put an end to it. I stole a glance at the Coxes who sat at the far end of the room. Their hands, unlike mine and Donald's, were not joined over the table, and there was silence between them. Mrs Cox was looking into her lap, and her husband was staring at the ceiling.

Both were clearly waiting for the end-of-visiting bell. The visit itself was a mere formality, and as such it would be repeated like a longstanding routine that has lost its original purpose.

'Has Cox been behaving himself?' I asked. 'After his last explosion?'

'They put him in solitary for a week,' Donald said. 'That calmed him down a little. Then they let him work in the garden.'

'I don't know why she visits him,' I said. 'He killed her mother.'

'He says he's innocent,' Donald said.

Don't you all? was on the tip of my tongue. But I refrained. I wanted evidence. I remembered that that had been the purpose of my visit. But I didn't know what questions to ask, and even if I did, I knew I wouldn't have the courage to ask them. 'How is the painting going?' I said instead. His answer would be safe.

He grew excited. 'They've asked me to paint a mural. In the games room. They've asked for a seascape.'

I was so happy for him. Alcatraz and Hollywood were not so far away after all. 'Have you started?' I was as excited as he.

'Tomorrow,' he said. 'They're getting me all the equipment.'

'Will I ever be able to see it?' I asked.

'They said something about a public day. Some bigwig to unveil it. Perhaps even the boys might come.'

It had been at least two visits since he had mentioned them, and I didn't know how to respond. Nothing on earth would induce them to come to a mural viewing. 'They might,' I lied. 'But even if they don't,' I added, 'they will be very proud.' I doubted that too. Pride belonged to another life and for them that life was over.

I looked across the room at the Coxes. I doubt that, throughout the visit, a single word had passed between them. She was still looking into her lap, and he towards the ceiling, and I saw them as an apt still-life in Donald's mural.

To my relief Donald did not mention the boys again, and I quickly pursued the topic of the mural.

'Do you make a sketch of it first?' I asked.

He seemed glad to discuss it and he launched into his plans. 'I'll have to measure the wall first,' he said. 'Halfway along it curves and I'll have to use that bend in the picture. I thought I might mask it in a rolling wave. So many colours in a wave,' he said. He was impatient. 'I can't wait to begin.' He has a life, I thought to myself. He has a purpose. He has more than I. Then I recalled my decision to cross-question him, but now in his mood of such cheer it would have been cruel perhaps to refer in any way to the reasons he was in this place, the reasons behind the innocence that he claimed. I was impatient for the signing-off bell. Again I looked over at the Coxes. There had been no movement between them. It seemed that they were set in concrete, rigid and unyielding, and I wondered how Mrs Cox would prise herself off the seat and make the bus. Then mercifully the bell rang and I rose.

'It goes so quickly, Donald,' I said, and I kissed him in my relief.

'You should take a holiday, sweetheart,' he said. 'Give yourself a break. I'm going to be busy here, and I don't mind if you miss a visit.'

I thought of the wooden leg and I felt myself blushing.

'I'm not a holiday person,' I said, having had bitter proof of that conclusion. 'I'll see you next time.'

On my way out, I passed the Coxes' table. She still sat there, unmoving. I dared to tap her on her shoulder.

'Coming?' I asked.

Then at last, she made a move. But a silent one. She turned away from him and took my arm while her axeman fixed his eyes on the ceiling.

'That's the last time,' Mrs Cox said, as we settled on the

bus, and I knew that I would be sitting next to her on the bus and the ferry, again and again. Even if her husband should die a natural and undeservedly peaceful death, she would still take the ferry and the bus, looking for a place to bury her pity.

By the time I reached home, I had made a decision. I had found myself unable to question Donald and I knew that I would never be able to do so. So I would make my own investigation. But I wasn't too sure what I had to investigate. Donald had told me often enough that he was innocent although the verdict had proved otherwise. But I could not bring myself to believe my Donald guilty. He had loved me for so many years and had shown his love in sundry ways. Night and day. How could I equate such a man with a murderer? And what kind of woman was I who could spend those years in such company? Donald *had* to be innocent, if only for my sake. Yet he had admitted to the killing of ten human beings – and declared in the same breath that he was innocent. Why ten? I asked myself. Why even one? And what does 'innocent' mean?

The doubts lingered. He must have had very solid reasons for doing what he did. It was those reasons that made him declare himself innocent, but nothing regarding them came out at the trial, and I hadn't dared ask him. Nobody on earth knew the 'why' of the crimes. Except Donald himself, and he would take those reasons to his grave. Why? Why? I kept asking myself. And I knew that it was in that 'why' that his innocence lay.

I did not know which way to turn. Had I known any of his family, perhaps they might have provided a clue. But he had no brothers or sisters, and his parents were dead. No nieces, no nephews for certain. But perhaps there were uncles, aunts or cousins. I knew there was a way of finding out. The name Dorricks must feature in the files of the Register of Births, Deaths and Marriages. But I baulked at such an idea. That would be a true invasion of Donald's privacy, and he would never forgive me. I was happy to put the idea aside and accept once more my Donald's innocence. So the 'why' was no longer viable.

Yet it nagged at me. But even if I were to approach a member of the jury or the judge, or Wilkins himself, they would have no answer. And why should they be in the least bit curious? Dorricks had killed, and on his own admission, stressing his innocence at the same time. But that rider they did not care to understand. They had put him away for life. He was off the streets and shrinks could go about their business without fear. That was their purpose, and justice had been seen to be done.

Yet the 'why' did not leave me. I decided to ask him direct. But not in person. Not to his face. I was too cowardly for that. In any case, I wanted to give him time to reflect, to arrange his answers. He would not want to be caught on the hop. So I decided to write him a letter. Letter writing is not my forte. Since he'd been in prison, I had written rarely. Just short notes to keep in touch. To let him know that he was in my thoughts and that he would never be forgotten. I started the letter with these assurances. Then I invented some street gossip. I told him that I had bought a new dress, which was true, and that I would wear it on my next visit. I described it in detail. All easy topics to write about. I was keeping the thorny subject till last. I thought I'd toss it off like an afterthought. Indeed I signed the letter with my love and kisses, then added a PS.

'I know you are innocent, my darling,' I wrote. 'That is what you say and I believe you. But sometimes I wonder why you did what you did. Why? That's the only part of this whole business that I don't understand. The reason for it all. And since I believe in your innocence, I think I'm entitled to know. Or maybe not. Perhaps it's none of my business, so you don't have to tell me if you don't want to. All my love, Verry.'

I noted that in the last sentence I had returned to the non-assertive Verry, that role in which I was at home. Three or four sentences of my self-assertion was more than I could hold, for that mood recalled the wooden leg and my humiliation. I underlined 'All my love', and put the letter in an envelope. It sat in my bag for the best part of a fortnight. I simply lacked the courage to post it. But my next visit was drawing near, and I knew I had to give him enough time to mull over his answers. I went shopping, because I didn't want to make a specific journey to the letter box. At the entrance to the supermarket, I turned my face away as I approached the letter box, then behind my back and when I wasn't looking, the letter was on its perilous way. I decided I didn't want to shop after all. I went home trembling, terrified of the consequences of what I had done. I tried to imagine how he would react. He might do a Cox on me and spend my visit in silence. Or he might ignore my letter and carry on as if he'd never received it. The latter was more likely, I thought. And that was what I hoped for, with all my heart.

I had a sudden urge to speak to my boys. I waited until the evening when they would be home from work. I needed their comforting voices. Their answering machine was crisp and clear.

'If you want to leave a message for Matthew or Martin Davies, please speak after the beep.'

At first I thought that I'd dialled the wrong number. I knew no one by the name of Davies. I had forgotten about the Davies alias. It was too painful to recall. Then I realised that I was utterly alone.

THE DIARY

EIGHT DOWN. ONE TO GO.

Or so I thought. But in truth, it's still seven down, and two to go. Because I cannot count the one I've just done. Because he doesn't fit in. My mistake. Human error. God forgive me.

I was so near to the end of my mission, that I suppose I became cocky. And over-ambitious. And so for my next attack – the one I'm not going to count – I really went over the top. I read in one of their trade journals about a symposium on psychotherapy methodology – whatever that means.

It was to take place in Hampstead Town Hall. Where else, since that is an area vibrating with psychobabble. It was to be an all-day session. And for an all-in fee, lunch would be provided. It didn't state whether or not it was open to the public, but I thought I might as well drop in, for there was no reason why I could not pass as one of them.

There was a goodly crowd, and I had no problem passing through the turnstile. I was faintly offended by my ease of passage, because I was not flattered by the assumption that I *was* one of them.

I took my seat at the back of the hall. It was a reasonably full row which pleased me because I didn't want to be conspicuous in any way. I checked on my gloves and the string in my pocket, and I settled down to listen to a paper discussing the treatment of geriatrics. I took out my little notebook, which I had brought to show willing, and I made a few illegible notes. I was very bored. I couldn't understand why people who had managed to survive into their old age should sully the rest of their lives with therapy which, even if it could lead them anywhere, would certainly require more time. I sat through the paper and joined in the clapping that followed. Then I had to sit through a number of questions from the floor. I had made no plans for anyone's dispatch. I simply thought it would be a happy hunting ground for my crusade. But naturally I had come armed.

In a lull between questions, I noticed a man rise from his seat and make for the exit. Presumably to find the toilet. It was too good to resist. I didn't know his name, or anything about him, but he was clearly one of them. So he would do. I slipped out of my seat and followed him. Those beside me were in eager discussion as they waited for the next question and they did not seem to notice my departure. I went through the exit door, and followed the directions to the toilets. They were on the lower floor, and as I descended I put on my gloves and fingered my string. There was an arrow which pointed to the Gents and I dutifully followed it. The door was ajar. I pressed it open. The stalls were on my left, and facing me was a row of sinks. He stood at one of them, washing his hands, and through the mirror he saw me enter. And he smiled at me. In all my crusade experience I found that death was often prologued by a smile. Unknowingly, of course, except to myself, and I always found it unnerving. And there it was again. Bright and open as if he were greeting a long-lost friend. I would not allow myself to return his smile. That would have been cruel. So I kept my stern regard and placed myself behind him. I knew I had to act quickly in case other so-called healers heard the call of nature, so I slipped the string around his neck. Then something extraordinary happened. I don't know how the man's terror manifested itself. Whether it melted his knees or astonished his bowels. I only know that I myself was close to collapse, having unavoidably confronted myself as a murderer. The mirror caught me in the act. Red-handed, and I could only thank God it was my one witness. I pulled tightly on the string, heard his gurgle, and I shoved his head into the sink. I avoided the mirror as I checked his pulse and I fled through the door, meeting no one on the stairs, and then slowly out of the place, gasping for air. I had to find somewhere to sit down. I was beside myself with horror. In all my killings hitherto, I had felt myself acting on another's behalf. Which was indeed true. I had never considered myself as a murderer. I was simply the servant of another. But now I had seen myself in the role, and I was appalled. I staggered to my car and drove to another area, far from the site of my haunting and gruesome reflection. I found a café about a mile away, and I ordered a large glass of iced water, hoping to dilute my shameful fever. I sat there for a while and tried to calm myself. I could not go straight home. Somewhere about my person, I bore the mark of Cain and I wanted to hide it from Verry. So I went to my office, my mirrorless office, where I could be alone. I sat at my desk and I noticed that I was still wearing my gloves. In my former killings, once clear of their sites, I had stripped them off my hands. Now the sight of them seemed like props in my murderer's role, that I had not been able to discard, as if they were a fitting accompaniment to my chosen career. But I hadn't chosen it. Not off my own bat. It was thrust upon me by circumstances, and to ignore it would have spelt betrayal. I had to think in this manner in an attempt to absolve myself of responsibility. But I knew it was futile. It was I who wielded the string. And of my own volition. My reflection in the mirror was irrefutable proof. I had murdered a man with my own hands.

But worse was to come. Much worse. As I was soon to

discover. I read about it in the newspapers. They revealed to me that his name was Theo Quick and that he was not a psychotherapist at all. He was a simple dentist, a profession with which I have no argument. It was his wife, with the misleading name of Joy, who was the guilty party. She was due to give a paper as part of the symposium, and her husband's good nature had sent him there to support her. He was an innocent. So I can't count him in. His murder would sully my crusade. So it's still seven down, and two to go.

But I can't leave it at that. Killing's not easy, even when the target is deserving. And poor Mr Quick had severely shaken my nerve. And it has called into question the whole moral purpose of my crusade. But I dare not have it questioned. There will be time for that and hopefully there will be no such time. Because there is no question that my crusade is just, and when doubts invade me, I have only to picture the rope and the shattered guitar. Those images acquit me of guilt, and they warrant each and every one of my sorties. I just wish that I hadn't caught myself at it. My murdering hands in the mirror was an image as indelible as the rope that had driven me to it.

So it's still

SEVEN DOWN. TWO TO GO.

God forgive me.

The symposium plodded along its weary way until lunchtime. Participants began to leave the hall and to adjourn to a committee room that had been arranged for a buffet. Outside the toilets below stairs, the queues formed quickly and moved in orderly fashion. That is, into the Ladies. But there seemed to be a hold-up at the Gents. And more than that. A total standstill. A cry was heard, a polite and very English male cry, which tried not to draw attention to itself, but at the same time needed to be heard. There was an equally polite response from those who were waiting, and someone at the head of the queue opened the door to view the cause of the alarm.

'Who is it?' he said.

'I don't know.' This from the finder. 'I can't see his face.'

'Is he dead?'

'I don't know. I don't want to touch anything.'

'Let's get a doctor,' another suggested.

A cry went out for a doctor. A real one, not the psychotherapist kind, and though the committee room was searched, while rumour blossomed, there was none to be found.

'Call the police,' someone suggested. 'It may be murder.'

Mrs Quick was looking for her husband, who was not among the buffet-crawlers. She presumed that he had gone to the Gents, and she prayed fervently that he was still in the queue. She made her way through the tables to see for herself. But he was not in the queue and there was hardly any point in asking whether he had been seen. Because he

167

was not one of them, and wouldn't have been known by anybody.

'I've got to see who it is,' she said, and she forced her way through the line. She was held back at the door.

'You mustn't go in there, Joy,' a colleague said. 'It's terrible.'

'It might be my husband,' she whispered. 'I have to see him.'

The man put his arm around her and led her towards the sink.

Mr Quick had slumped. His head was hooked on the rim of the sink, and his long torso had slipped its length on the tiled floor. There was blood everywhere, along with the poor man's waste. Joy screamed when she saw him. She didn't need to see his face. She knew his stance. It was the one he assumed as he stretched over to kiss their son good-night.

'It's Theo,' she said. 'What have they done to him?'

She was led screaming from the room. Her colleague took her up the stairs and sat her in the foyer. Somebody brought a glass of brandy, as rumour of his name and the manner of his passing rumbled around the hall.

'The police are on their way,' someone said.

It was Wilkins' deputy who answered the phone.

'Good news,' he said to his boss. 'Another shrink. He's done it again.' He expected a whoop of joy from his boss, a cry always heard when the killer had struck yet again. Another chance to trap him. But Wilkins responded only with a sigh, a sigh of regret, not only for the victim but for his poor self. Yes, it certainly was another chance, he thought, but a chance simply to prove his incompetence yet again. He was certain there would be no prints and no witnesses. He simply wanted no part of it. Ever.

'Why don't you go?' he said to his deputy. 'See what you can find.'

'Alone?' the deputy asked.

'Take the usual squad with you, of course,' Wilkins said.

'I mean, without you?' The deputy could not believe the request.

'Why not?' Wilkins said. He sighed. 'I'm not up to it any more.'

'Rubbish,' the deputy said. 'You're the only one who can handle it. You've been unlucky, that's all. And that's no reflection on your efficiency. I'm not going without you.'

Wilkins smiled. He was grateful for such loyalty. He rose wearily from his desk. 'Let's go,' he said.

The chairman of the conference had suggested that no one should leave the hall. 'I'm sure the police will want to talk to you,' he said.

And so they milled around, their appetites seemingly uncurbed, as the buffet spread was consumed and the drink ran dry.

On arrival at the hall, Wilkins sent his deputy to talk to the audience and to ask witnesses to come forward. Apart from Mr Quick, was anybody seen leaving the hall before the interval? Was anyone seen to be acting strangely? And, even as the deputy put the questions, he fully expected a negative response.

A few delegates had approached the platform, he was told – those with written questions – but nobody was seen to leave the hall. And no one had been acting strangely – as if such a question made any sense to a bunch of shrinks to whom everybody, except themselves, was strange and in dire need of treatment.

Wilkins fared little better below stairs. He found what he expected to find. The guitar-string garrotte. And unsurprisingly he found no prints. Anywhere. He ordered the body to be taken away for further examination, though he knew that no amount of further examination could unlock the mystery. When he heard that the victim was not even a psychotherapist, he found the news encouraging. The killer was slipping. He might never risk it again. But still he would be left with eight guitar strings on his back-burner, a severe blight on his reputation and a sure barrier to any hopes of promotion. Before leaving the hall, he went to see the grieving widow. No murder was fair game, but this one was grossly unjust. Poor Mr Quick was guilty of nothing. He was a simple dentist, and in no way qualified as a victim. But he was dead, and his wife undeniably a widow, and Wilkins was overwhelmed by the sheer unfairness of it all. He spent some time with Mrs Quick. A silent time. He was moved to hold her hand and he hoped that that gesture would do for the words he couldn't find.

As was his wont, he went to Mr Quick's funeral in the vain hope of finding the stranger. More often than not in murder cases, the killer would skirt the grave out of some ghoulish need to see his job well and truly done. But the shrink killer clearly had no such need, and Wilkins wondered what lunatic appetite prompted his carnage. If that were known, it would be a clue of a kind. If it were a simple loathing of the profession itself, he could well have planted a bomb in the symposium and killed a hundred birds with one stone. But it was more than that. It was something to do with the guitar string. That was the key. And with such a weapon, one could only kill one at a time. He thought of discussing this proposition with Dr Arbuthnot, but his reliance on that source was fast dwindling. He decided instead to pay a visit to the United Kingdom Council of Psychotherapists and thought regretfully that he should have involved them at a much earlier stage. He didn't know what help he could expect from them, but he was clutching at straws.

The director welcomed him and wondered why his visit was so tardy.

'I didn't think you could help me,' Wilkins said. 'These killings are strictly police work, and often to involve outsiders clouds the issue.'

'But we're hardly outsiders,' the director said. 'Our whole profession is at risk.'

Wilkins agreed with him and was contrite. 'I'm sorry,' he said. 'I should have come sooner.'

'We want to help and we think we can,' the director said. 'We have made a decision, that is, the board and I. It seems that this killer has had very easy access to our practitioners. He had simply to make an appointment which was granted. We have now sent out a directive to all our members to the effect that no new patients can be taken on to their lists without a written recommendation from their general practitioner. Those new patients must be examined before recommendation is put forward. We think that might help stop him in his tracks. It will at least be a hindrance.'

Wilkins considered himself incredibly stupid. It was a move that he himself should have suggested to the Council after the very first killing. 'I'm grateful,' was all that he could say.

On his way back to the station, he mulled over their decision. But for some reason, he was not entirely satisfied. The Council's decision might well protect its own members.

But there were hundreds of unqualified therapists out there, practising all kinds of dubious therapies and they, if the killer was not too picky, would be equally at risk. He could only hope that his killer would have some respect for professional qualifications.

He reported the Council's directive to his deputy but he too, though welcoming it, had similar doubts.

'We must press on,' he said. 'This time the killer has slipped. He's losing his touch, and he may well be frightened. And that's how we're going to catch him. By his fear.'

Wilkins saw no sense in such an argument. He regarded it simply as a token of encouragement. 'Let's hope you're right,' he said.

Today is visiting day and I'm dreading it. He will have received my letter. He will have considered it, or more than likely, he will have torn it up. I'm sorry I ever sent it. You see, despite my doubts, I always look forward to seeing Donald. I miss him. He was my best friend. I miss our evenings together, when we used to sit side by side on the sofa, watching television. We never talked much. That's why he loved the box. You wouldn't notice our silences. But I never minded them. There was always somebody else around to talk to. We were happy together and that's all that mattered. Cosy. How many married couples could say that?

So, despite my fears, I was looking forward to seeing him. Mrs Cox too. I was sure she'd be on the ferry, despite her declaration that she would never visit her husband again. I was sorry for her. Had my husband murdered my mother, I would have washed my hands of him, but she probably thought the same of me, and wondered why I visited still. And, sure enough, she was in her usual compartment on the train and she was clearly as glad to see me as I her.

'Here we go again,' she said. It was her customary greeting, followed by the usual rider. 'I don't know why we keep on doing it.'

I let it lie. We were accidental friends, and such friends should waste no time in argument.

'I've brought him a jigsaw,' she said. 'A rose garden. He'll like that. It'll give him something to do during our visit. Instead of staring at the ceiling.'

'And what will you do?' I asked.

'I'll watch him,' she said.

'You could do it together,' I suggested.

'He'd kill me if I touched it,' she said.

And I believed her. His sentence to prison had certainly saved her life. 'Do you write letters to your husband?' I asked her. 'Between visits?'

'I write almost every day,' she said.

I was surprised and slightly irritated by her submission. A daily letter was overdoing it a little. 'Why so often?' I asked.

'It's safer,' she said. 'I can say what I like and he can't strike me through the post. I vent all my anger before each visit. Then I'm happy to sit back and look at him.'

It seemed to me then that her visits were punitive. Her letters were slaps in his face and she simply visited him to watch him squirm. Then I remembered my own letter, and again I was afraid.

Mrs Cox seemed to be in a very good mood, and from what she had told me I presumed that her current letters had not minced words. As we boarded the ferry, she made straight for the bar and ordered a double whisky. I stuck to orange juice. I had a feeling that by the end of the ferry crossing she would need my support. We settled ourselves by the window and watched Portsmouth recede. She was suddenly talkative. She'd taken herself to see a musical, and she outlined the plot for me, even contributing a couple of songs.

'If I'm going to sing,' she said, 'I need to wet my whistle,' and off she went to the bar again, returning with two glasses, each bearing a double whisky. I hoped that one of them was not for me. But I needn't have worried. She set the two of them in front of her and once more started to sing. She refuelled herself from time to time, as her voice strayed off key, and her speech slurred. By the time we reached Fishbourne, she was legless. I helped her on to the bus. She was roaring with laughter, interrupted by attempted snatches of song. I rather hoped she might be sick, so that she could sober up a little before the visit. But she showed no signs of nausea. Indeed she became more and more merry as we neared the prison.

I dreaded our entrance. We reached the gates and she made no attempt to pull herself together. In any case, she was too far gone. And she knew it.

'I'm drunk,' she shouted. 'And I bloody well don't care.'

I steadied her into the visitors room where the axe-man was waiting. He noted her merriment and in no way did it please him. How dare she be merry, he thought, while I'm stuck in here with no fun at all. He rose but made no move to help her to her seat, so that I had to hang on to her till the last moment. I moved the seat towards her and sat her down. Then I pushed the seat towards the table and let her get on with it. Whatever the 'it' was.

The other inmates and visitors were staring at her and she was going to give them a run for their money.

'What the fuck are you all staring at?' she shouted. 'Let's all have a sing-song. Cheer up this bloody place for a bit.' Then she started on a carol as if it were Christmas. The others stared at her, marvelling or disgusted. Some of them actually joined in the singing. 'Good King Wenceslas,' they sang and even the warder who stood warily at the door could not help but mouth the words. And at the point when the snow lay round about, Mrs Cox shovelled it aside and threw up a glorious fountain of vomit. Its matter spread across the floor and the room was suddenly silent and ashamed. The warder crossed the floor to where Mrs Cox stood. Gently he took her by the arm.

'Let's go now, shall we?' he said. 'Let's get some air.' He led her outside, and shortly a cleaner appeared with bucket and mop; soon all disgusting traces of Mrs Cox's statement had disappeared.

'Poor woman,' I said to Donald. And I did indeed pity her. Mrs Cox was a prim lady, middle class and respectable, her mouth a stranger to blasphemy. Her swear-laden discharge was a cry for help, and she had had to drink herself into a stupor in order to utter it. I wondered what state I would find her in when the visit was over.

The visitors room was unusually quiet. Mrs Cox's outburst seemed to have stunned them all into silence. Remembering my letter, I was glad of it, and I hoped that Donald would make no mention of it at all. Then out of the silence, and as if it came from another place, I heard, 'I got your letter. And your PS,' he added. 'It doesn't matter why I did it,' he said. 'At least not to anybody else. It only matters to me. And that's why I'm innocent.'

I didn't know how to respond. But I knew I couldn't let it lie.

'Why doesn't it matter to me?' I asked. 'I'm your wife. Surely I'm entitled to know.' I felt the interference of that assertive 'Verry' and I knew that there would be a price to pay.

'You are not entitled to know,' he shouted.

It was the first time I could ever remember that Donald

had raised his voice to me. A vein of rage throbbed in his forehead.

'You are *not* entitled to know,' he said again. 'It was *my* crusade and you had no part in it.'

How often he had used that word during his trial. 'My crusade', or sometimes, he varied it with 'my mission'. What it meant was nobody's business but his own. It encapsulated the whole of the 'why', the 'why' of his total innocence. I had been given my answer, which was no answer at all, and I had to be satisfied.

'I'm sorry I shouted at you,' he said, and he squeezed my hand. 'But I want you to understand, sweetheart. My crusade was sacred to me. Holy almost, and its cause can never be shared. Because of its cause, I am innocent. And I ask you to believe me.'

'I do,' I said helplessly, but I'd have been happpier if he'd given me just one simple reason to believe that he was not guilty. I had hoped to find it in the 'why', for that's where it undoubtedly lay, but I was clearly not to be privy to it.

I felt he was anxious to change the subject, so I asked him about the mural.

'I've started,' he said eagerly. 'At least, I've done a rough design on paper. The Governor has seen it and he's given the go-ahead. Verry,' he said, squeezing my hand once more, 'I'm so happy.'

I wondered whether he had ever been so happy in the whole of his life and the thought caused me to ponder whether he needed me in his life any more. Whether he, like his two sons, had put the past behind him and found a different way, as they had done. And where did that leave me, with no role at all, except that of a sad observer waiting in the wings for a change that would never occur? And like Mrs Cox, I asked myself whether there was any point in visiting him at all. But without my visits, my life would have been stripped of its punctuation, and Mrs Cox's likewise, and together we would travel the train, the ferry and the bus, if only for the sorry sake of grammar.

'Tell me about the design,' I said.

'It's dominated by the sea, of course. I think water will resonate for all of us here. We live on an island and the sea is our only escape. It is also our confinement. So we are obsessed with it.'

He smiled at me. 'D'you understand?' he said.

'Of course,' I said. And I did. Every syllable of it. He was going to paint his childhood at the sea and it was only of secondary importance that it would be meaningful to others. It was *his* childhood, as it had been *his* mission, *his* crusade. He was a loner, my Donald. Through and through, and I wondered whether ever in his life he had shared himself with anybody. It was on the tip of my tongue to ask him. In my bones, I felt it would be a clue to the 'why'. But I'd learned my lesson and I held my tongue. But I did dare to ask whether there would be people in the mural.

'Yes,' he said. 'But just vague figures. Just suggestions of faces. They won't have any prominence.'

That made sense, I thought. For Donald, other people were mere gestures.

Then, as always, I was relieved when the bell rang the end of visiting time. I was uncertain of my place in the scheme of things. Of them all, Donald and my boys, I was the only one who had not found an alternative way. I was miserable, and the sight of Mrs Cox, hiding in the back of the bus, in no way cheered me. We were a wretched and silent pair all the way back to London. Occasionally she muttered 'never again' but it had become a mantra recited on all her return journeys.

'See you next time,' I said, as I left her at Waterloo. That was my mantra too.

I was glad that Donald seemed to have found some form of happiness. He'd been happy enough when we'd been together. But sometimes he'd get depressed and the mood would last for days. I tried to talk to him about it, to find out what was the matter. But he was silent. Angrily silent. So I didn't ask any more.

Once there was a Christmas concert at the boys' school. End of term thing. The boys were in the school choir. We both love carols, Donald and I, and we went to cheer the boys. There were going to be a number of turns. There was no programme, so the headmaster announced each performer. The concert started with a short nativity play by the juniors. Then a young boy, about twelve he was, played the piano. And he was really good. I often wonder what became of him. Then there were carols and Donald took hold of my arm, and I heard him singing along under his breath. He was happy then. Occasionally he would squeeze my hand and I would respond. I remember we were happy. Both of us. And at the same time.

But it was not to last. I shiver now when I think about it. After the carols, the headmaster announced the last item of the concert. He promised us a treat. The performer was the pride of the school. He had been awarded a scholarship to the Royal Academy of Music. The board was deeply impressed with his prodigious talent.

'Ladies and gentlemen,' he said. 'Trevor Hope.'

And on came Trevor. He was a handsome lad. Smiling. Over-smiling, perhaps, to cover his nerves. He gripped his guitar under his arm. He made for the stool, centre stage, and rested the guitar on his lap. At last he seemed to relax. The smile faded, and as he dropped his fingers on to the strings, he closed his eyes and began. And it was then that Donald snatched his hand out of mine, and I felt him shiver beside me. He could have been moved by the boy's playing, but Trevor had hardly started. I couldn't understand it. I tried to take his hand, but he pulled it away. I stared at Trevor and tried to concentrate on the music. It was so beautiful that for a while I was lost in it as were the rest of the audience, who sat in awed silence. So when the slightest sound broke that silence, it was like thunder. And it came from beside me in the form of a sob. I dared to look at him and I saw tears rolling down his cheeks. He was racked with sorrow. I prayed that the recital would soon be over and that the applause would drown his weeping. And when it mercifully came, I was the first to put my hands together to cheer that young boy who seemed to have broken Donald's heart. The applause lasted for some while, and I prayed that there would be no encore.

Trevor left the stage, and the headmaster once again took the platform. He thanked us all for coming, and reminded us of the collection that would go to the fund for Christmas gifts in the local children's home. The audience began to leave. I took Donald's arm. He was calm. He wiped his face and put on a brave smile. Instinctively I knew that I should never, but never, make any reference to his disturbance. And I never did. But I kept remembering it, and on my way back home from the prison that day it attained a dazzling clarity in my mind. And I wondered whether it was part of that elusive 'why' that I was seeking.

THE DIARY

STILL SEVEN DOWN. TWO TO GO.

I've never read this diary. I've written it. That's all. And when
it is finished, when my crusade is done, I shall throw it in
the fire. It is for no one's reading. Not even my own. In truth,
I am afraid of it. For there are times when the purpose of
my mission and its compulsion, there are times when they
blur and almost fade: the attic, the rope, the kicked-over stool,
the shattered guitar, all those images of my crusade; sometimes I wonder whether I have dreamed them all. It is because
of those moments of loss of faith that I am afraid to read this
diary. I've only two more to go. Though I think of it as one.
Because the ultimate call will not be random. It has been in
my sights since the very beginning. I know its address. I know
whom I shall see, I know exactly what I shall say. And all of
it gloveless, for what happens after that won't matter any
more. I will have conquered and I will have found my peace.

But there's the rub. And that's why I delay. Why I postpone that final *coup de grâce*. It's because I fear that the peace
I have been seeking all these years will elude me, because its
price has been so monumentally high. So I delay. I shall spend
my time reinforcing those images of my cause. I shall dwell
in that attic, glued like a limpet to its door and I shall view
the hopeless overturned stool, the shattered guitar and the
rope. And I shall shut my eyes on what the rope cradles.
Thus I will nurture my purpose, invigorate my resolve, and
all will be well. I shall cease to be a murderer.

But poor Mr Quick still bothers me. No amount of righteous motive can justify his careless dispatch. I say to myself

it was human error, but the word 'human' sits uneasily in that context. It was a mindless and brutal murder. When this is all over, I shall seek out Mrs Quick and offer, for what they are worth, my profound apologies. For then I shall be at peace with myself. I shall have honoured that pledge, the pledge that I made to myself all those years ago, the pledge that I swore on that attic threshold.

It took me some years to start on my crusade. I was not lacking in resolve. Or even courage. My enemy was procrastination. My marriage to Emma was one cause of the delay. I simply didn't trust her enough. She was a born questioner, and I could hide nothing from her. All I could give her was my silence, a silence filled with plans awaiting process. Then she left me and Verry happened. Verry, who found my silence normal and was not given by nature to questioning. And it was her total acceptance of everything I did and didn't do, of everything I said and didn't say, it was that acknowledgement that allowed me my first sortie. Thereafter, I seemed to be wholly licensed.

And as I plied my pledge, my boys were growing into men. Today is their graduation. They have both done well in their exams and they have gained places in a school for business studies. They want to go into banking. They are so alike, my boys, and so loving to me and Verry and to each other. We're taking them out tonight to celebrate. They've chosen a French restaurant. They went on a school trip to Paris last year and they were deeply impressed by the food. We spoil them, Verry and I. And why not? There is nothing on earth that is a substitute for parental love. And nothing on earth that can better that love between siblings. And I ought to know.

As we sat around the table, joking and laughing, I wondered what they would think of their father's crusade. One day, of course, they will learn about it and I pray that they will under-stand and forgive me. That they will know that their father is no murderer but one who loved, was loyal, and one intent on settling accounts.

We returned home late, too late to make arrangements for another sortie. But I was not tired. Verry and the boys went to bed but I stayed up, imaging, standing at that attic door, renewing my pledge.

STILL SEVEN DOWN. TWO TO GO.

W ilkins considered that the move from the Council of Psychotherapists had paid off. The shrink-killer was lying low. Or perhaps he had even done with his gruesome trade, having acknowledged defeat. He took comfort in the thought that at least there would be no more victims, even if the threat to their lives still remained at large. From time to time, he reviewed the threadbare accounts of the killer's tally. Eight in all, but all his rereading revealed no clue. The French had unsurprisingly drawn a blank on Mademoiselle Lacroix, though they had put up a fine show. They had arrested and eventually freed seven suspects, despite having no evidence against any of them. They just wanted to be seen to be hot on the trail. But there are back-burners in Paris too, and that is where Mademoiselle Lacroix reposed, and would remain until Wilkins broke the barrier. For he was still convinced that the French murder was the work of the man he was seeking. But for now there was little he could do. He would have to wait until, and if, the killer struck again. Wilkins would be given another chance and though he prayed for it, he prayed equally for an end to the killings.

The station was not busy. It was holiday time, and even felons seemed to be on vacation. There were the usual muggings and break-ins, but those fell outside Wilkins' remit. They were part of the duties of lesser officers. Even his deputy was on holiday, and Wilkins looked forward to his return, so that he himself could take a break. Perhaps they would go to the Lake District again; it was within easy calling reach of London. For wherever he was, Wilkins felt himself on duty.

He was idling with *The Times* crossword when his telephone rang. It was the duty officer. He reported an attempted murder at a house in Hampstead. An ambulance was on its way, and a man was being held.

'You seem to have sewn it all up,' Wilkins said. 'Why do you need me?'

'I don't know,' the officer said. 'The policeman on the site said it was one of your cases.'

Wilkins called for his car and reached for his coat. It was not quite murder. And a man was being held. That didn't necessarily make it one of his cases. He was curious. There was something missing. Some information to which he was not privy. Until he arrived at the scene.

The victim, he was told, was one Charles Mills, a psychotherapist. So it was clearly one of his cases. A man had been taken to the station. He had openly confessed to the attempted murder. He was found with the gun smoking in his hand. 'An absolute nutter,' the policeman said.

The victim had been taken to hospital. Wilkins ordered the front garden to be sealed. It was there that the gunman had loitered, waiting for his victim's arival. The car was in the driveway, and Mr Mills had been shot getting out of it. There had been no attempt at escape. The shot had been heard and there was no shortage of witnesses. Moreover, there was a confession. Wilkins no longer needed fingerprints. But on his way back to the station, he wondered whether it was one of his cases, after all. If it was, then his killer had slipped mightily. Because of the Council's directive, he'd not been able to make one of his usual appointments. And he was desperate. He'd come out into the open. But what didn't make sense was his change of weapon.

He was anxious to get back to the station and begin the interrogation. He chose a woman police officer to sit by his side in the interview room. A woman's presence during such a procedure was always useful. It could embarrass the subject or intimidate him, and that subject would find both unnerving. Wilkins studied the suspect carefully. He seemed to be a man in his forties, though Wilkins would not have been surprised if he'd been much younger, for his face was creased with worry lines which etched his haggard expression. He was tall and gaunt and, despite his clothes which were of the finest cut, and his air of wealth, he looked as though he could do with a good meal. He was not as Wilkins had imagined *his* man. *His* killer was short, stocky perhaps, ugly and bald. Nothing like the man who sat before him.

'Is he going to die?' the man asked.

It was a perfectly natural question, Wilkins thought. The man was simply concerned whether he would be tried for murder or grievous bodily harm.

'We don't know as yet,' Wilkins said.

'I hope he does,' the man said. 'He deserves to. After all he's done.'

But Wilkins would come to that later. He needed the simple facts of the assault. Its reasons could be explained when those facts were made clear. He switched on the tape.

'State your name,' he said.

'Thomas Rhys May.'

'Age?'

'Thirty-one.'

'Occupation?'

'Psychotherapist.'

Wilkins shivered. He thought of Dr Arbuthnot who had suggested an unfrocked shrink as the killer. Was this Mr May one of those struck off the register? His hopes rose once more. He saw his overcrowded back-burner quickly unpeopled. A slate wiped clean. He smiled. He suddenly loved Mr May. He would go easy with him for a while. He could afford to.

'Just answer the questions,' he said. 'Tell me what happened. In your own words. Just the facts.'

'I was waiting for him,' Mr May said. 'I knew he went every Thursday to work at a private clinic. Well, he would, wouldn't he, money-grubbing bastard? I knew what time he came home and how he parked his car in the drive. I'd watched him at it a number of times. So I decided to do it today. I hid behind the hedge in the front garden, and I waited. He arrived on time, as expected. I stayed hidden until he got out of the car, then I came out from behind the hedge and faced him. I wanted him to recognise me. I wanted him to know who was going to put him away.

'"Thomas?" he said. He seemed surprised because in no way was he expecting me. He must have noticed the gun in my hand. Then I saw the fear on his face and I was delighted. I let him indulge his terror for a little while. There was a sudden puddle of it at his feet. Poor bugger raised his hands. Where did he think he was? On the Somme? But I don't take prisoners. So I shot him. That's it. I've confessed. What more d'you want to know?'

The facts were now clear. Mr May seemed to have held nothing back.

'Have you done anything like this before?' Wilkins asked.

He still clung to the hope that the man was the killer he sought.

Mr May looked offended. 'Of course not,' he said. 'Do you think I make a habit of this sort of thing? Like that notorious shrink-killer? Now he's a *real* nutter and I don't know what his reasons are. But I had a reason. I had just one target. Mr Mills. If he doesn't die, then I hope that I've at least crippled him for life. Just as he's done to me.'

'And what has he done to you?' Wilkins was patient. He already suspected the answer. He'd heard it before during his investigations.

'I've told you,' Mr May said. 'He's crippled me for life.'

'In which way?' Wilkins asked.

'It's a long story and I don't expect you to understand.'

'I'll try,' Wilkins said.

'Any chance of a cup of tea?' Mr May asked.

'With pleasure,' Wilkins said. He was going to indulge this man. He was going to spoil him. Despite his denial of the other killings, he smelt his guilt across the table. His posh accent and smart clothes could not save him. Slowly and very gently he would wear him down.

He switched off the tape, and asked the policewoman to organise a cup of tea. 'And a biscuit perhaps,' he added. Then he himself left the room. Once outside, he rehearsed the questions that he would ask. And their tone. Especially their tone. How they would begin in a voice of such understanding, and how gradually they would lose their gentle edge. Until in a burst of rage, he would openly accuse him of serial killing. Then the blessed charge. 'I am arresting you, and so on and so on.' The press would be alerted, and those stupid gendarmes across the water. Then he and Mary could go off to the Lake District once more, or even abroad perhaps, for he no longer needed to be within call.

Shortly the policewoman arrived with the mug of tea and a wrapped biscuit, and together they re-entered the interview room.

Mr May was smoking a cigarette. He seemed calm and at peace with himself. Not for much longer, Wilkins thought. May took the mug of tea with a smile. 'Just what the doctor ordered,' he said. 'I'm parched.'

Wilkins switched on the tape, and announced the time of the renewed interview.

'Shall we go on?' he said. 'You were going to tell me in which way Mr Mills has crippled your life.'

Mr May leaned back in his chair and took a large gulp of tea.

'Are you married, Inspector?' he asked.

'I'm asking the questions here,' Wilkins said gently. 'But to answer your question, and there must be no more, yes, I am married. Married twenty-six years.'

'Children?' Mr May persisted.

'I have two,' Wilkins said. 'Now, can we get on with it?'

'It's important for me to know if you are married,' Mr May said. 'Because if you are, you are more likely to understand my position.'

'Explain yourself,' Wilkins said.

'I'm married,' Mr May said. 'Twelve years. Three children. And now all that is over.'

He took another gulp of tea. Wilkins noticed that the man was losing his calm. His hand was shaking as he held the cup. Wilkins was confident of a further confession. Shooting Mr Mills was only the beginning. Or the end maybe. Either way, he would urge him to backtrack. He would drive him to Mr Winston's door, then to Angela Mayling's, to Bronwen Hughes', to Alistair Morris's and to all the other doors he had entered. He would put that guitar string back in his gloved hand. He would grind him down until he was broken. Until he whispered that he had killed them all. But he had to be patient. The man wanted to talk about his marriage. He would listen, feigning sympathy, though he knew that the state of the man's marriage was irrelevant.

'You seemed troubled, Mr May,' he said. 'Why is your marriage over?'

'Can I ask you another question?' Mr May said.

Why not? Wilkins thought. He could afford to play with him a little longer. 'Go ahead,' he said.

'If you found out that your wife was sleeping with another man, what would you do?'

'I would be very sad,' Wilkins said.

'Is that all? Sad?' Mr May's voice was raised. 'Sad,' he said with a sneer. 'What kind of man are you? Wouldn't you do something about it?'

'Like what?' Wilkins asked.

'Like a gun,' Mr May said. He had begun to tremble.

And so had Wilkins as all his hopes faded. As all his certainties melted. As his holiday was reduced to mere fantasy, and as all hopes of promotion collapsed. He had been called in to investigate a simple domestic, one that with little trouble could be proved. He had a sudden urge to strike Mr May for his honesty and for the rude shattering of his dreams.

'Charles Mills was sleeping with my wife,' Mr May was saying. 'She was going to leave me and take the children with her. You ask her. You ask him. If he's still alive. He knows why I wanted to kill him. He knew it when he saw my gun. He's ruined my life. I hope he pays for it.'

Then Mr May finally broke down. 'I had to do it,' he mumbled. 'I couldn't help myself.'

But Wilkins felt no pity for him. 'Charge him,' he told the policewoman. 'Grievous bodily harm. And that's for starters. Then read him his rights.'

He left the room. He had never before felt so dejected. So let down. His killer, his *real* killer must be laughing his head off. He could tick off yet another shrink for nothing. If not dead, then certainly wounded. One more to add to his tally of revenge. One for free. How much longer could it go on, he wondered.

Once back at his desk, he rang the hospital to enquire as to the condition of Charles Mills. He would survive, the doctor told him, though he would take some weeks to recover. His wife was at his bedside.

Wilkins wondered what on earth they could find to say to each other. He felt a sudden urge to ring his wife, just to hear her voice, just to know that she was at home and possibly preparing his supper. He was floundering and he desperately needed anchorage.

I had a letter from Donald this week. He's full of excite-ment. The mural is almost finished, and the Governor has given him permission to show it to me on my next visit. I'm a bit nervous. I'm sure I will like it and I'll certainly say so. But I'm still nervous. Not for myself. I'm nervous for Donald. For what comes after the mural? How will he deal with the anti-climax when the mural is finished and unveiled? What then for my Donald? But I must not think about that. I must manage one day at a time. As he will have to do. I told my boys about the painting, and their indifference was sublime. I have to accept that they will never see him again. I think of the last time they laid eyes on him. And he on them. It was the final day of the trial. The verdict had been given. He'd been sentenced to life and he was being led away from the dock. He turned and looked towards the gallery where I was sitting with my boys. He stood still and waved his hand. I could see that he was trying desperately to give us a smile. But it was hard for him. And I know why. Because at that moment, my boys, both of them at the same time, rose from their seats and turned away. Then I saw Donald shrug helplessly and wave again, but he knew that that wave was for me alone.

But I don't want to think about the trial. It's too depressing. Though no doubt there will come a time when I'll have to relive it, if only in my search for the 'why' of it all.

I bought a new dress for my next visit. The unveiling I

was promised called for a display. I wanted Donald to be proud of me. I thought of Mrs Cox and I was uneasy. She would be without me in the visitors room, silent with her axeman, while I would be enjoying myself elsewhere. I hoped that she wouldn't be envious, and as a result our accidental friendship would be frayed.

She was not on the train when I boarded, and I half hoped that she had kept her word and decided not to come. But at the last moment I saw her rushing down the platform and there she was beside me, breathless and already tearful. But sober.

'I wasn't going to come,' she said. 'I tried to stop myself. But I couldn't. So here we go again.'

I took her hand. 'You would have regretted it,' I said. 'I'm glad you're here.'

'I'm still not sure I'll go,' she said, though the train had already pulled out of the station.

Then we were silent. We had only one train conversation, and both of us were tired of it. Once on the ferry, she went straight to the bar, and I dreaded the outcome. She returned to our table, but she was not carrying glasses. Instead, she held a half-bottle of whisky which she stuffed into her bag. Alcohol was not allowed into Parkhurst and I wondered what she had in mind.

When we disembarked from the ferry, we walked together to the waiting bus. But as we reached it, she stopped. 'I'm not going,' she said. There was no hesitation in her voice, so I knew there was no point in trying to dissuade her.

'What will you do?' I asked.

'I'll sit by the sea,' she said. 'I'll just look at the water.' She opened her bag and tapped the bottle. 'This'll be good company,' she said.

I feared for her and I wondered how she would get back to London.

'When shall I see you?' I asked.

'I'll make my own way,' she said, and she was already off, and at a brisk pace, as if she feared I would hold her back. But I did not go after her. Her decision was her own business and I boarded the bus alone.

As I entered the visitors room, I saw the axeman rise and move towards me. He was used to seeing us arrive together.

'Where is she?' he shouted.

'I'm not your wife's keeper,' I shouted back. 'I don't know where she is.'

'Was she on the bus?' He was now quite close to me.

'No,' I said. And that was true. I just hoped he wasn't going to enquire about the ferry.

Donald was coming towards me, and I was glad of his protection, for the axeman was threatening. A warder approached him and tried to calm him down. Then he led him out of the room. At the door he turned.

'Bitch. Fucking bitch,' he announced to the assembly. He could have been referring to me or to his wife. It was probably the same phrase he'd used to his mother-in-law before he axed her. His curse was directed against women in general. He simply hated them.

I was trembling when I sat down. Donald held my hand. I leaned over and whispered to him Mrs Cox's whereabouts and her likely condition.

'I don't blame her,' he said. 'She's better off there than here. At least she's safer. He's a monster.' He smiled at me. 'You will be honest when you see it, won't you?' he said. 'Tell me what you really think.'

'Of course,' I said. 'Though I'm sure it's wonderful.'

'Let's go then.' He led me out of the room, past the empty Cox table which looked no more vacant than when the wretched pair were sitting there. Donald took my hand and led me through endless corridors. He was excited and in a hurry and I trotted by his side. On our way we passed a patrolling warder. He nodded to Donald. 'Ten minutes,' he said. Donald was clearly a 'trusty'. At last we reached the games room. I hoped there'd be no one inside so that Donald and I could have a really private view. But as he opened the door, I saw a man leaning over the pool table, lining up a shot. He was alone, and he didn't have to turn around. For I knew from his axeman's back exactly who he was.

'Let's go,' I whispered to Donald.

'He won't bother us,' Donald said. 'And this is your only chance.'

The mural was on the opposite wall, and I could see it from where I stood. But not in detail. In the long view it was impressive enough, and I wanted to move towards it to examine it closely. But to cross the room meant skirting the pool table. There was no way we could avoid being seen. But he must have heard the door closing behind us and he turned around.

'Ignore him,' Donald whispered.

But the axeman would not be ignored. All his life he had been neglected, disregarded, overlooked, and he was damned if, even in prison, doing his time, the pattern would be repeated.

'What d'you think?' he sneered. 'Awful, isn't it? A kid could do better than that. Just a load of green paint. And we're supposed to be grateful for it.'

We ignored him as Donald urged me towards the wall.

Our backs were towards him, and I wasn't happy. Suddenly he was at my side, the billiard cue in his hand. I thought he might strike me and I wanted to run.

'You know where my wife is,' he said. 'She always comes with you.'

'Not this time,' I said.

He raised his cue, and my Donald went for him. I knew that Donald was no match for the axeman, and I ran from the room shouting, 'Help, help.'

A warder came running.

'There's a fight in the games room,' I said.

He ran and I followed him. As he opened the door, I heard an ominous silence within. I would have preferred some noise of life, of struggle even, and I dreaded what I would find. Then I heard the sound of a potted billiard ball and I saw the axeman bent over the table as we had first found him. Getting on with his game as if nothing had happened. But that 'nothing' lay on the floor. I ran to him and knelt by his side. I could see no blood and I was relieved.

'I'm all right,' Donald said. 'I'm all right. Just a bit of a headache.' He was clutching his temple where he'd obviously been struck. The warder knelt beside him.

'OK, Dorricks?' he said. 'Stay there. I'll be back.'

'Take that monster with you,' I said.

He smiled. 'Leave him to me.'

I watched him take Cox by the scruff of the neck and drag him out of the room.

'I'm all right, I'm all right,' Donald kept saying. 'Look at the painting. Tell me what you think.'

I went to the wall and studied it. Its detail was overwhelming. The curve of every wave, the single water-drops of every ripple, the corrugated sand ridges on the shore. In the wide expanse of water, I counted at least six separate shades of green, with here and there a hint of blue and towards the shoreline, a froth of beige. I was dazzled by its beauty, a grand sweep of brush-laden love.

'It's beautiful,' I said. I moved along the wall towards the curve. He had masked it in rocks, a cluster of them, rugged, and of varying heights. On top of one of the ridges were two figures. Little boys with linked arms. I looked closely, but there were no known definable features. Just two figures in a seascape and it seemed to me that he had drawn our boys, but being so unsure of them, he'd had little confidence in their features.

He had risen from the floor and now he stood by my side.

'It's wonderful, Donald,' I said. 'Every square inch of it.'

He put his arm around my shoulder.

'Are those our boys on the rock?' I dared to ask.

'Perhaps,' he said, and he took away his hand.

The 'perhaps' worried me, coupled as it was with that gesture. I wondered what was behind that 'perhaps' and whether it was related to the 'why' I was seeking. I knew in my bones that they were linked.

I heard the end-of-visiting bell, and as it rang, a warder came into the room.

'Beautiful isn't it, Mrs Dorricks?' he said.

I nodded. Sad too, I thought. For the painting was so free, so unconfined, so unfettered, yet its setting was limbo and durance vile.

'Let's have the nurse look at your head,' the warder said. 'An early night is what you need, Dorricks, and a couple of aspirins. You don't have to worry about Cox,' he added. 'He's back in solitary.'

Serves him right, I thought, though I knew that his solitary would only increase his wife's pity.

I took Donald's arm and the three of us walked down the corridor.

'It's absolutely beautiful,' I said again. 'Are you going to be all right?'

'Don't worry, Mrs Dorricks,' the warder said. 'He needs to sleep. I'll let him call you in the morning.'

I took Donald in my arms. 'You've made me very happy,' I said.

But on my way back to the ferry, I wasn't happy at all. The image of those two little boys on the rocks nagged at me. That 'perhaps' image. Donald's melancholy and his uncertainty saddened me. Yet the mural had been beautiful and I had to ignore its setting, and view it only for itself.

When we reached Fishbourne, I looked around the pier for Mrs Cox. There was no sign of her, and I was glad of it, because I didn't want to be the one to break the news about solitary. I presumed she'd finished off her bottle and taken an earlier ferry. I travelled alone back to London and made an early night. But I couldn't sleep, and when I did, in short snatches, it was only to dream of rocks on the curve of the wall and the 'perhaps' figures on their crests.

I rose early and made myself breakfast, though I wasn't hungry. But it was something to do, something to occupy me until Donald's phone call.

It came at eight o'clock. He sounded perky and assured me that he was well. That no damage had been done. I told him once again how much I loved his picture.

'You make my day,' he said.

I told him that there had been no sign of Mrs Cox at the ferry. That she must have taken an earlier crossing.

'She didn't,' Donald said. 'She showed up at the prison at about ten o'clock. Drunk as a lord. Banging on the gates. Wanting to visit. They sent her away. The warder told me this morning.'

'Poor woman,' I said. She couldn't resist it, I thought, and I imagined her sitting by the water, drinking herself silly, then dragging her unwilling feet to visit a man she didn't want to see. Yet she could not help herself.

'I hope she got home in one piece,' Donald was saying.

'No doubt I'll see her next visit,' I said.

'I have to go now,' he said. 'Thanks, sweetheart, for everything. I'm innocent, you know. The mural proves it.'

I wondered what he meant by proof. And I knew that those 'perhaps' boys on the rocks had something to do with it. But I was as confused as I had been from the very beginning. That beginning when the verdict had been given. Sometimes I think I am never meant to understand it. That Donald is protecting me from some unpalatable truth. My fear is that I shall die in that same ignorance, and it would be such a waste. But I don't know how to proceed. It seems I have no choice but to embrace that ignorance and to know that it is good for me.

It was early enough, I thought, to ring the boys before they left for work. Matthew answered the phone.

'We were just leaving,' he said. Then, 'I love you, Mum.'

'Me too,' Martin contributed.

'Thanks,' I said. It was all I wanted. The Margate seas were calm again, and my boys were fishing off the rocks.

THE DIARY

EIGHT DOWN. ONE TO GO.

No more procrastination. No more shilly-shallying. I must prepare my next sortie. The attic images are fixed in my eye. No adjournment will shift them from my retina. I take out my directory. Since I am approaching the end of my crusade, I feel like taking a flying leap. I have not forgotten the thrill of Paris, that so random strike. But I will not risk the continent again. I scan my register. Believe it or not, there is one lone practitioner on the Isle of Eigg. A Mr Scott, way up in the Hebrides. With a sparse population, surrounded by water, unreachable for parts of the year, they must all be pretty doolally to start with. And with only one therapist to hand, they must keep him pretty busy. On the other hand, the state of doolalliness on Eigg might be considered the norm, in which case Mr Scott would be sorely unemployed. But with luck, either way, he might find time for me. It would mean a flight. And a ferry. So as far as Verry was concerned, it had to be Devon once again. I made the usual call and asked for an appointment.

'Have you seen your doctor?' Mr Scott asked.

I couldn't see that that was any of his business and I told him, 'No. Why should I?'

'I need a doctor's letter of referral,' he said. 'I cannot see a patient out of the blue.'

Well, bugger you, I thought. If you're so picky, I'll try someone else. There are plenty of other therapists crying out for business.

I was rather sorry about Eigg, but I still fancied an island.

201

I thought the Isle of Wight might oblige. There were a number registered in that location, and I chose a Mrs Tomkins. I made my usual telephone call.

Mrs Tomkins' secretary answered, and when I asked for an appointment, she had the nerve to ask me the name of my GP.

'Why is that necessary?' I asked her.

'Before I make an appointment for you, I need a letter of referral from your doctor. He must examine you before an appointment can be made.'

'Thank you,' I said. 'I'll go and see him.' Then I put the phone down.

I contacted three more therapists and had to endure the same response. I was at my wits' end. Only two more to go. Or in real terms, only one, because I expected no such difficulty with the last of my crusade. I sensed a conspiracy of sorts, and I suspected Wilkins' hand behind it. I tried not to be alarmed. Seven times in my mission I had been lucky. I must not be greedy. I must find another way.

Since it was now clear to me that the register of qualified therapists was out of my reach, I had to find another source. Other so-called healers. Unqualified and legion. But letters after a name did not guarantee competence. And I should know. I went to a London suburb and bought the local paper.

There were two back pages of services. The first column was devoted to rubbish disposal, and as a natural corollary, as it were, there followed a column under the heading of 'Alternative Healing'. The sundry practitioners offered a variety of services, from Positive Thinking, whatever that was, to Energy Boosting, Hypnotherapy, and Stress Counselling. I thought the last would suit my purposes and was closest to that on offer from the professionals. I returned to my office and made my usual call.

Her name was Penny Brown, and she couldn't have cared less about my GP and his referral. I gave her a false name and arranged to call on her the following afternoon. I decided that this one was not going to be a quickie. I was curious about Miss Brown's methods. I would wear a mackintosh to avoid fibre in case I chose to sit down. And, of course, my gloves. I can't understand why anybody wants to be cured of stress. A life without stress must be very boring indeed, because such a life dare not allow itself to be fed by the imagination. For it is that very gift that causes stress and I'd far sooner accommodate the anxiety that ensues than forgo the talent of imagination. But each to his own. Miss Brown clearly thought that stress was bad for you and I was fascinated to discover how she thought it could be remedied. I rather looked forward to our meeting, and I hoped that I wouldn't warm towards her.

I didn't have to use my Devon ploy. Miss Brown lived in Surbiton and I could be there and back within a couple of hours.

It was raining when I set out, and I was glad of it, for it legitimised the waterproof that I was wearing, and once inside, I had no intention of taking it off. Or my gloves. Both would pass as the uniform of a stress-riddled loner, in dire need of counselling.

Miss Brown herself answered the door. She was a middle-aged woman, too young to die, but I could not afford such a thought and at the sight of her, I imaged that attic again, and the rope, and I duly stepped inside her parlour. There was a pervading smell of incense, sandalwood, and I wondered whether that played a part in stress counselling.

'Sit down,' she invited me.

'I'd rather stand,' I said. 'I'm restless.'

'Well, take off your coat then,' she suggested.

'No. I feel unsure without it.' I had all the qualifications for her counselling.

'Would you like me to stand too?' she asked.

'No,' I said quickly. I needed her sitting for my dispatch. 'But thanks for asking. I appreciate your willingness to join me in my troubles.'

I was a willing patient and she seemed anxious to help.

'Is there anything special that is troubling you?' she asked.

'Yes,' I answered with absolute honesty. 'But I can't talk about it.'

'Can you give me any clue at all? Jealousy, perhaps? Greed?' She was way off the mark. I shook my head.

'Is there any name that comes to mind?' she asked. 'Some name that has to do with what is troubling you.'

I nodded. 'There is a name,' I said. But only because I didn't want to disappoint her. Any name would do, I thought. I was about to pick one out of the hat, when she interrupted.

'Don't tell me the name,' she said. 'I want you to tell it to yourself. Over and over again. I want you to tell it to that wall. Over there.'

She pointed to a corner of the room where a large punchbag was fixed to the adjoining walls. It was a big red bulk of cushion and looked solid enough. It invited assault.

'Stand in front of it,' she said. 'And start punching. Say the name to it, over and over again.'

It was as if she was asking me to play with her. Like a child. And on that basis, I obliged. I started to punch the bag, gently at first. And rhythmically. One two, one two. And a strange feeling overcame me, a feeling of welcome release. I went on punching with a certain pleasure, but I noticed that my punches obeyed no rhythm and that they were strong,

angry and almost violent. I punched away. I was sweating
and I heard a groan from my mouth. A word was forming
under my tongue, claiming release, and it seemed I could not
hinder its escape. I was losing control and punching my heart
out.

And then it came. The name. In a whisper at first, as if I
didn't want to hear it. But louder and louder, indifferent to
audience. 'Robinson,' it yelled. 'Robinson.' Over and over
again, in dire dactyl trisyllable.

'That's enough,' I heard Penny shouting from where she
sat. I looked at her, listening still to the harsh echo of that
terrible name, and I pitied her. Pitied her profoundly. I might
well have let her off my hook, due to her kindness and skill.
And skill indeed it was, for at the price of a mere ten quid,
and with no letters after her name, she had unleashed a name
that had haunted me for almost thirty terrible years. But now,
bless her, she knew too much. She knew the name and she
would have to go. Apart from the inhuman error of Mr Quick
at the symposium, the death of dear Penny Brown was the
only one I would live to regret. She had done me great service
but the knowledge that I had shared with her was to be her
own undoing.

I swallowed my remorse, and rushed behind her.

'What are you doing?' she asked, and with a smile as if
I was about to play a silly trick on her. Those were Penny's
last words. I choked them with my string, checked her pulse,
and watched her die. But I didn't flee from the room as was
my habit. I tarried awhile and told her I was sorry. That
she was but an accidental station on my crusading road and
that if there were a heaven, she had certainly earned her
admission.

I left the house, and once outside I took off my waterproof

and gloves. It had stopped raining and I noticed a rainbow in the sky. Its beauty did not please me. I was dejected. Penny Brown had not been an easy dispatch, because in many ways she had been good to me. She had mightily eased that last attack of mine, the killing that would justify them all and, hopefully and at last, bring me peace.

I drove home slowly. In time, Wilkins would be driving in the opposite direction. That journey would be buoyed with hope, and the return with dire disappointment. I was beginning to feel sorry for him. Indeed, I was beginning to feel sorry for everybody, not least for myself. And once again I questioned the need for my crusade, punctuated as it was with doubts and uncertainties. And, worst of all, with scruple. Then I imaged the attic again, the rope, the shattered guitar, and slowly my doubts dissolved. 'I am innocent,' I said to myself. Over and over again. Only one more to go, and the hardest of them all. But it would be the righteous justification of all that had gone before. I dreaded it, but I would rejoice when it was all over.

EIGHT DOWN. ONE TO GO.

The clerk at the station switchboard picked up the emergency line.

'She's dead,' a woman screamed at him.

'Slow down, lady,' the clerk said. 'First tell me your name and where you're speaking from.'

'More than dead,' she kept yelling. 'Murdered.'

'What is your name, madam?' The clerk was patient.

'Mary Stone,' the woman said. 'I'm her flatmate.'

'And the name of your flatmate?'

'Penny Brown. But she's been murdered.'

'Give me your address, Miss Stone. And don't touch anything.'

'Thirty-three Wallace Way,' the woman whispered. 'Come quick.'

'We'll be there,' the clerk said and instantly set the wheels in motion.

Wilkins was one of those wheels. From the clerk's scanty report, it sounded like a run-of-the-mill murder. It would make a change. He would expect prints, a break-in perhaps and a handful of witnesses. Such a change was a relief to him and he almost looked forward to its investigation.

Until he reached Wallace Way and saw the guitar string.

'What did the victim do?' he asked wearily, though he already knew the answer.

'She was a therapist,' the flatmate offered. 'Alternative.'

But the 'alternative' had not saved her. Wilkins' world collapsed. He had to sit down as he realised that the directive from the Council had failed. The killer had found pastures adjacent, but new. There would be no end of it. He couldn't even be bothered to check for prints, for signs of a break-in or even for witnesses. He knew he would draw a blank on them all. He waited for the pathologist's assessment, which bored him with its repetition. Then he ordered the body to be taken away. He delegated officers to the usual house-to-house inquiry. Miss Brown lived in a flat in a converted Victorian house and there were comings and goings all the time. No one conspicuous had been seen. The coroner's report was more or less a copy of all his others.

He rang the Council of Psychotherapists and told them of the latest development. They were as devastated as he.

'Have you any idea,' he asked them, 'how many people out there are practising alternative therapy?'

No. They had no idea, but suspected they were legion. They had no advice to offer. The ball was in his court, they said. And with some irritation, they remarked on his failure rate. Wilkins didn't need their criticism, and he put down the phone more dejected than ever. He fully expected a summons from his superior calling for his resignation. So he made some excuse to his deputy and went home. On top of all my incompetence, he thought, I am also a coward. As he opened the front door of his house, he smelt the homely odour of baking bread. Friday was Mary's bread day. He felt bound to count his blessings. A good wife, a fine home, his children settled, retirement was a seductive option. They could travel abroad, enlarge their horizons, have time for hobbies. Hobbies? he thought. I have no hobbies. My work is my hobby and my hobby my work. Early retirement was unthinkable.

'You're early,' he heard Mary call from the kitchen. 'Do you want some lunch?'

'No,' he said quickly. 'Just popped in for some papers. Another murder, I'm afraid.'

'Shrink?' Mary asked.

'Not quite,' he said. 'But close. An alternative therapist. Unqualified. But obviously qualified enough for his purpose. It could go on for ever.'

She knew better than to ask if there were any clues. Mary had lived with the killer alongside her husband. She knew every detail of the man's activities. She had shared her husband's hopes and disappointments, to the extent that she almost shared his responsibility. There was nothing she could offer him. Except lunch.

'Sit down,' she said. 'A salad, a piece of strong cheddar, and a glass of red wine. It won't do you any harm.'

He was tempted. But lunch at home would be a rehearsal for retirement, and he knew that he would miss the station canteen. He would miss its gossip, its speculation, its camaraderie. He had to face yet another failure, and take the consequences, whatever they might be. To be taken off the shrink case would certainly afford a measure of relief, but at the same time, he would fight his lone corner to persevere.

He went to Miss Brown's funeral. And looked for the stranger. Of all the shrink funerals he had attended, this was the most crowded. And the most unconventional. Miss Brown lay in a cardboard coffin, which was painted with red and yellow chrysanthemums. The chapel was lined with scented candles, and a live rock band sat on the platform. Friend after friend spoke of Miss Brown as a healer, enabler and, above all, as a loyal friend. She had enriched many lives and would be truly missed. The band played and they sang her favourite songs. It was more of a concert than a funeral, an almost happy celebration. Yet its aftermath was the saddest of all. Wilkins stayed in the chapel long after the mourners had gone and once again he resolved never to leave his post until he could hold that monstrous killer and put him clean away.

Me again. I keep thinking of poor Mrs Cox. I see her banging at the gates of the prison, holding on to them for fear of falling in a drunken stupor. I see her turning away, down the path that leads to the road. And then I lose her. I wonder how she got back to the ferry or whether she even made it at all. I have to wait another week before my next visit, and half of its purpose will be to see Mrs Cox. I am drawn towards her without quite knowing why. We have nothing in common except for husbands in stir. But that's all I need to have in common with anybody. There is nothing else in my life that so preoccupies me. Because I think about it all the time. Like Mrs Cox, I wonder why I visit him, and like her I am confused. Our cases are not that different. Both our husbands were found guilty and both proclaimed their innocence. But there the likeness ends. Mr Cox was found with a bloodied axe in his hand and with his headless mother-in-law at his feet. Hardly a picture of innocence. Whereas my Donald was found clean and at home, minding his own business. And weaponless. In my mind I have no doubt about Mr Cox's guilt, and he says he's innocent because he has to join the common chorus of Parkhurst. But is my Donald singing too? And for the same reason? I think of the trial and how he admitted his guilt to every murder, but claimed in the same breath that he was innocent.

I wasn't at home when he was arrested, I'd gone out for the evening with the boys. We'd been to the cinema and, for the life of me, I can't remember the film. Donald doesn't like the cinema so he stayed at home. He said he had work to do. We came back late, and Donald wasn't in the house. It didn't bother me. He often went out for a late-night walk. To clear his head, he used to say. It was about eleven o'clock when the phone rang. It was Donald, ringing from the police station. 'I'm innocent,' were his first words.

'What are you talking about?' I asked him.

'I've been arrested,' he said. 'I'm at the station. Will you come? I need overnight things. And don't tell the boys.'

'Why have they arrested you?' I had to ask.

'I'm innocent,' he said again.

Then he put the phone down.

'Who was that?' Matthew asked. 'What's happened?' He could see from my trembling that all was not well.

So I told them. I had to. I could think of no excuse for running out at that time of night with pyjamas in my hand. They were stunned. Unbelieving.

'Shall we come with you?' they asked. I told them no, but that they should wait up until I returned. I packed an overnight bag with Donald's things and took a taxi to the station.

I was not allowed to see him alone. He was in a cell and a policeman stood in the corner. We whispered to each other, but we were still overheard.

'What's the charge?' I asked him. 'What are you supposed to have done?' My use of 'supposed' declared me on his innocent side.

'Murder,' he said. 'Ten murders. They'll try me for one. The last one, but I shall ask for the others to be taken into consideration.'

I thought 'consideration' was an odd word. Did it make

him more or less innocent? I started to cry. 'I don't believe it,' I said. 'What happens now?'

'I'm in court tomorrow morning,' he said. 'I don't suppose I'll get bail. I'll be on remand until the trial.' He seemed so matter-of-fact about it all, as if he himself had organised its production. 'I'll see a solicitor before the hearing,' he added, 'and then we'll take it from there.'

'Take what?' I asked. I couldn't believe a word of what he was saying.

'My innocence,' he said.

'Of course,' I said.

Then another officer came to the cell and told me I had to leave. I held Donald in my arms. 'Don't worry,' I said. 'It's all a terrible mistake. I'll see you tomorrow.'

I was glad to leave and find some place to sift through my thoughts, to pinch myself awake from what I considered to be a bad dream. But I was not in bed. I was sitting on a bench outside the police station, wide awake. And thunderstruck. I asked myself *when* he could have committed those crimes. I knew where he was most of the time. He was in his office or he was at home. He simply didn't have *time* to do anything else. And surely I would have noticed some change in him. He was sometimes depressed, sometimes elated, but that was the norm with him. I was convinced that somebody somewhere had made a terrible mistake.

The boys were waiting up for me. I couldn't fob them off with excuses. Tomorrow, after the hearing, they would find out anyway. So I told them all I knew. 'He keeps saying he's innocent,' I told them.

'Of course he is,' they said. 'They've just got the wrong man.'

I was glad of their support, shortlived as it turned out to be. None of us slept that night. We kept meeting each other in the kitchen, making tea. We could hardly wait for the morning and the hearing that would prove a monumental error.

People were queuing outside the court, baying for blood. I wanted to kill them all. I pushed my way into the courtroom, with my boys in tow. Donald was already seated in the dock, flanked by two policemen. He was talking to a man who stood below him. I presumed that the man was his lawyer. When they had finished speaking, Donald looked around the court, and I raised my hand hoping he would spot me. But he clearly could not decipher me among the crowd. The hearing lasted only fifteen minutes. Donald was asked to state his name and his address, and then the charges were read out. 'Rubbish,' I heard the boys mutter, and an indignant 'shush' came from those who sat near us. 'That's his wife,' I heard one of them say. 'Two of a kind, I reckon,' her companion said. I felt no need to defend myself. We *were* two of a kind, Donald and I. And both innocent. The magistrate then asked Donald how he pleaded. 'Not guilty,' he said. Bail was not even asked for. Such a request on such a charge would have been laughed out of court. He was committed for trial at the Old Bailey in two months' time.

As we left the court, the boys and I, we were ambushed by photographers. I don't know how they knew who we were, why we were any different from the other spectators, but word must have gone around that we were kin. I was furious, mainly for the boys' sake. They were embarrassed and tried to hide their faces. I suggested they should go away. They could stay with my cousin Frieda in Scotland.

They could lie low there until the trial began, and their father's innocence could be proved.

They agreed to go, but reluctantly, wishing to stay for my support. But at the time, I needed to be alone, for it was then, after the hearing, that my doubts began to surface, together with my certainty of his innocence and I needed to be alone in my confusion.

I went to see him, of course, while he was on remand. He seemed strangely cheerful. He had no complaints, he said. He was being treated well. Then he began to laugh. I asked him what was so funny and he said that a psychiatrist had been sent to examine him. 'I gave him pretty short shrift,' he said. 'I told him to find himself a more honest and less damaging career. I told him to stuff it and, knowing my history, I think he was mightily relieved to get away.'

Because Donald seemed so unworried, I pretended to share his optimism. He kept insisting on his innocence.

The second time I visited him on remand it was to learn that he had dispensed with the services of his lawyer. He told me he was going to defend himself. It didn't seem like a very good idea to me. If he were innocent, as he kept claiming, he would need the support of professional skill to prove it. 'Why have you sent him away?' I asked.

'He doesn't believe what I tell him. I tell him that I certainly have killed, but that I am innocent. He just refuses to understand it.'

'I don't quite understand it myself,' I said.

'I don't expect you to understand it,' he said. 'I don't expect *anybody* to understand it. I just want people to believe me. I am guilty of murder, but I am innocent, and I don't have to explain why.'

215

It struck me that a judge and jury would not be entirely satisfied with such a confession. But I said nothing.

'You just have to believe me,' Donald kept saying. I was angry with him and I wanted to demand reasons why I should believe him, but I looked at him sitting there, confined, and I knew he didn't need my anger. And it was then that pity sprouted, and that, together with my doubts, apt companions, have dogged my days and nights since the verdict.

We went to the trial every day, me and my boys, but I have to confess, I remember very little about it. And understood even less. Donald spoke for himself and made no attempt to clarify his plea. He said he had indeed killed Miss Robinson but that he was innocent. He asked for nine other murders to be taken into consideration, and he admitted with total honesty that he had killed them all. Yet I am innocent, he kept protesting. When asked if he could explain his innocence, and give some reason for the killings, he simply said, 'I was protesting against a profession that is corrupt, that in the name of healing cripples, damages and threatens life itself. That is my protest, a protest for which I make no apology. You have to believe me.' His answers would have tried the patience of Job.

I knew that the trial would not last for very long. People were getting tired of Donald's refusal to explain. His protest was not acceptable. The verdict could only go against him even if only on the basis of the jury's irritation. It was not surprising when it came. Guilty. And a life sentence.

Almost a week later, after making their arrangements, my boys left home. It took me some weeks to accept that I was a grass widow and very long grass at that. Since then, I serve my sentence along with Donald, which is why I think constantly of Mrs Cox who is doing exactly the same. And though either of us could be liberated at any time, neither of us can deal with such pity-laden freedom. Drunk or sober, Mrs Cox will be on the train, the ferry and the bus and I shall be by her side, because we cannot help ourselves.

THE DIARY

EIGHT DOWN. ONE TO GO.

I think of those weary, sturdy, determined mountaineers who climb Everest. There must come a moment when the summit is in their sights. Do they sit for a while and wonder? That spot where they will hoist their triumphant flag is more than visible. It beckons. Yet still they sit and wonder. They wonder about the aftermath. They wonder about the anticlimax. They are rooted to their penultimate station, because they are afraid. I wonder what gives them the courage to risk arrival. Or rather the courage to acknowledge that they have no choice. I sit here and I wonder. I waver and I falter. I am infirm of purpose and I know that the last sortie needs must be. And, in truth, I am terrified.

Those mountaineers, they climb, and no doubt with each step they are beset, like myself, by doubts and uncertainties. But there the likeness ends. For I have scruples, and they have none. But I think to myself that I have had scruples before, that my conscience has pricked at almost every station. Yet I have endured. Yet I have proceeded. But now, in sight of my goal, that same conscience paralyses me.

I am tempted to recap on my run of luck, itemising each attack, but that would only serve to further a delay, perhaps a total withdrawal, even though there is only one strike to travel. So I image again: that attic, that rope, that overturned stool and that shattered guitar, and I think that if ever I were to complete my mission, and in spite of it, those pictures would never fade. So I sit here, writing in my diary, postponing, delaying, stalling, while my hand sweats with fear.

I wonder how I must pass the time, but then I know that time is too precious to pass. I think I might write down an account of my climax. How I shall dress for the visit, what route I shall take to the house, how I shall enter, and what I shall say. It will not be a quickie. Not this one. It will take time, for I have much to explain. There will be little dialogue. I myself shall hold the floor. But then I think that should I write it all down the very writing would excuse me from doing it. That putting it all down would be enough. I would have said it and my words would be as good as the action. They would do. It is tempting. But it is a coward's way. I must steel myself. My crusade, every step of which has been so meticulously planned, oh so righteously deserved, that crusade must not, at its last port of call, be abandoned. But now at least, I have acknowledged that I have no choice. In my mind I have acknowledged it. But the distance between the mind and the heart is immeasurable. I pray sometimes, but I don't know to whom and even less do I know why. All I know is that in that attic, all those years ago, God's back was turned.

EIGHT DOWN. ONE TO GO.

The death of Penny Brown had shaken the police department. Rank and file. For all could deduce its horrendous implications. The killer was choosy no more. Almost anybody was fair game. No one was more aware of this than Wilkins himself. He sat at his desk in utter helplessness, not knowing where to turn. All he could do was to wait for the call from his superior.

When it came, he was almost relieved. He was weary of blind alleys, of absent witnesses, of evaporated prints. He was beaten, and all the evidence, or lack of it, pointed to his defeat. Yet he didn't consider that anybody else on the station could have done any better and this thought heartened him a little as he made his way to the Chief Superintendent's office.

Chief Superintendent Billings was welcoming. He offered him coffee, insisted on it almost, as if to delay the matter of their meeting. As he poured, he asked after Mrs Wilkins and the children. Then he asked if he had a holiday in mind.

'You've been working overtime, Wilkins,' he said. He was homing in on his target, sideways as it were. 'Do you have any hobbies?' he asked. It was as if he were preparing an obituary before his subject was dead.

Wilkins put down his coffee cup. 'Get to the point sir,' he said.

'Well, I'll give it to you straight,' Billings said. 'You've worked well. You've done your very best. But I think we need a new approach. So I'm promoting you to Chief Inspector. You're a good officer, Wilkins, and you've done great service. I want you as my assistant. More pay, of course, and more generous leave. How do you feel about that?'

A desk job, was all that Wilkins could feel. The saving on shoe leather seemed its only advantage.

'Who will replace me?' he asked.

'Evans, your deputy,' Billings said.

'He's a good man,' Wilkins said. 'And loyal. But he'll need a stroke of luck. He'll have to wait for the killer's mistake. As I have done. Tell me, Chief,' he asked, 'could I have done anything different?'

'You did everything you could,' Billings said. 'I don't expect any quick results under Evans. It's simply a question of shifting the burden on to another's shoulders. I would have imagined, Wilkins, that you would be almost relieved.'

'Of course, there is a measure of relief,' Wilkins said. 'But I'll miss the chase. It's become almost an obsession.'

'That's the point,' Billings said. 'Obsessions can be dangerous. They can cloud the issue. Not that they have done in your case, since you've been given very little issue to cloud. The shrink killer is an almost invisible man. It may take years to track him down. I'm doing you a favour,' Billings said.

Gratitude was in order. But how could he be grateful to be given the chance of sitting on his backside for the rest of his service days?

'When do I start?' Wilkins asked wearily.

'Take a few days off,' Billings said. 'Then come in on Monday of next week. I'll have a comfortable office waiting for you. Can we have a drink on it?' he asked. He was already uncorking a bottle from his cabinet. 'Let's drink to a long and happy partnership.' He poured two glasses which both men raised to the toast. Wilkins drank, but more to swallow the lump in his throat than to celebrate his so-called promotion.

He went back to his office, and he was glad to find it unoccupied, that his deputy had not already moved in and assumed his status. When he heard the knock on the door, he knew it was Evans. 'Come in,' he called, suddenly pleased with company.

'What can I say?' Evans asked. 'Except that I'm sorry.'

'Sorry for what?' Wilkins laughed. 'Sorry for my removal, or for the buck that passes to you?'

'Both,' Evans said. 'I can't do any better than you have. That I know. And I don't look forward to it. But I'll miss you. Won't be seeing you in the canteen any more. You'll be dining posh with the bigwigs.'

'And I'll be sitting at my desk in my posh office all day, writing out reports.'

Both men laughed. Each would no doubt miss the other. Evans sat down. There was clearly something he wanted to say. He leaned forward. 'Inspector,' he said.

'You can call me James now,' Wilkins said.

'Thank you, sir,' Evans said. 'I just want you to know that if anything happens of interest, any evidence of any kind in the shrink killings, I want you to know that I'll inform you immediately, and you'll be back on the case. Even if on the quiet.'

'I'm grateful to you,' Wilkins said, 'and I hope for all our sakes that you will call on me soon.'

When he reached home, he broke the news to his wife. He sensed her feelings would be as mixed as his own. So he was surprised when she expressed her delight. She would no longer have to share his false hopes and disappointments.

'But I have failed,' he protested.

'Rubbish,' she said. 'You've done everything you could. You've had no leads to follow. Not in all these years. He'll never be caught, that killer. He's one step ahead and always will be. You're well rid of him. We're going to celebrate.' She took a bottle of champagne from the cabinet. 'I've been saving this for a special occasion, and I can't think of anything more special.'

Her delight cheered him. 'I've got a few days' leave,' he said. 'Shall we go away?'

'Let's go back to that Manor House,' Mary suggested. 'It's so cosy there. D'you remember that nice couple we met and had dinner with? Dorricks or something. I wish I'd taken their address. Then I could have kept in touch with them.'

'Perhaps they'll be there again,' Wilkins said. 'But in any case, we'll have some leisure time together.'

'I'll drink to that,' Mary said. 'And to many more week-ends. It's a new life for us, James.'

'We'll have to invest in evening dress. Both of us. There'll be lots of official dinners.' He counted his blessings, and toasted them. But privately he drank to his erstwhile deputy, and his promise to include him in the kill.

Me again. Ver-ine. I'm off to my punctuation. To my prison visit. I shall see Mrs Cox again. I shall not mention her last visit or the fact that I know about the late drunken call to the prison. She might volunteer it herself, and hopefully laugh about it. For no reason that I could fathom, I was feeling cheerful myself. I looked forward to another view of the mural, if that were allowed, and to sharing invented gossip with Donald if time were to hang heavily on our hands.

Mrs Cox was already seated in the train. And to my relief she was sober. And she looked contrite.

'I'm going to be a good girl today,' she said as I took my seat opposite her.

Such a pity, I thought. Mrs Cox was far more interesting as a bad girl, but that was a mean thought and I suppressed it.

'He's been in solitary again,' she said. 'I don't know why.'

But I did, and was certainly not going to tell her.

'Fighting, I suppose,' she said. 'It'll be the death of him, that violence.' She said it with a smile, a wishful-thinking smile, and I could not help but join her.

'I haven't brought him anything,' she said.

'Neither have I,' I told her. It's hard to bring gifts for people who have everything, which in a sense they do, though both men, in truth, have nothing, a nothing which no amount of presents could augment.

Her axeman was seated as we entered, and he was already

looking at the ceiling and would probably continue to do so for the length of the visit. Donald was at his table too. He was not looking at the ceiling, but staring at nothing, as if in a trance. He did not look well, and my heart rushed out to him.

'What's the matter?' I said as I sat down.

He didn't even look at me. I took his hand. 'Are you not well?' I asked.

'I'm a bit low today,' he said. And then he looked at me, as if I were a stranger.

'It's me,' I said. 'Verry. What's the matter with you?'

'It's a bad day,' he said. 'I get them sometimes.'

'Anything in particular?' I asked.

'Nothing,' he said.

'Is the mural finished?'

'Yes,' he said tonelessly. 'And they want me to continue it on to the ceiling.'

'But that's wonderful, Donald,' I said. 'They must be very happy with it. It'll be like the Sistine Chapel.' I've never been to Rome, but I've read about that ceiling. Seen a film of it too. 'Have you started it?' I asked.

'Don't want to,' he said.

'But why? It's a great opportunity.'

'For what?' he asked. His voice was raised. 'An opportunity to paint a ceiling. And maybe another ceiling. And maybe another wall. What kind of life is that? What kind of future?'

I had no answer to that one.

'I might as well be dead,' he said.

I squeezed his hand. 'Don't talk like that, Donald,' I said. 'What will I do without you?'

'I'll never get out of this place,' he said.

'You will. I promise. After a few years, you'll get parole. They'll take your paintings into acount. You've done them a service.' I listened to the rubbish I was talking. Donald was right. He was unlikely to get parole. Ever. And he knew it.

I wondered what had brought on this sudden depression.

'Are you especially worried about anything?' I asked.

'I think of you a lot,' he said. 'I wonder what you do at home. All by yourself.'

'I keep busy,' I said.

'Has the house changed? Have you moved furniture? Changed the rooms?'

I sensed that he was leading up to some question that he was afraid to ask.

'I've changed nothing,' I said. 'It's exactly the same as it was when you were there.'

'Are you going to stay there?' he asked. 'Or d'you think of moving? Packing everything up.'

'No,' I said. 'I'm staying where I am. And I'll be there when you come out.'

I was still waiting for the question that I knew he wanted to ask. And then it came.

'Are my clothes still there?' he asked.

'Of course,' I said. 'Where else should they be?'

'Verry,' he said, 'I want you to promise me something.'

'What?' I asked.

'I know it sounds stupid. I just don't want you to give my clothes away. To Oxfam or something. Those shops are for dead people's clothes.'

But I knew he was asking for more than that. He was not asking me to keep his clothes. He was asking me to keep out of his wardrobe. And I wish he hadn't. I hadn't opened his wardrobe door since he had left. That cupboard was his and private. But now he had suggested that it contained more than mere clothes. That it might house an answer to the 'why' that I sought. I would have to restrain myself. But I knew that it was a temptation that was irresistible.

'Promise me,' he said again.

I squeezed his hand and hoped that that would satisfy him.

He cheered up a little then. 'Promise me in return that you'll do the ceiling,' I said. 'It will take your mind off things.'

He nodded.

I wished the bell would ring. God forgive me, but I was anxious to get home to open that wardrobe door. I looked across at the Cox table and was not surprised to find her looking into her lap, and her axeman staring at the ceiling. It seemed an awfully long way to come to exchange a sullen silence. And I hoped for her sake, as well as for my own, that the bell would quickly send us both away.

But somehow I had to fill the time that was left to us. 'Have you decided on a design for the ceiling?' I asked.

'It has to be the horizon,' he said, 'limiting the sea on the wall. And birds,' he said. 'And clouds, I think. The rollers in the sky.'

'I can't wait to see it,' I said. Then the bell rang.

It seemed that Donald was as relieved as I was, for he rose from his seat as the bell was still tolling.

'I'll take you to the door,' he said.

Mrs Cox still sat there, as if reluctant to break the silence. When she saw me, she rose, took my arm, and we left the room together.

'Good God,' she said once outside, 'it's a relief to open my mouth. I couldn't find a single word to say to him. Nor he to me. This is positively my very last visit.'

I'd heard it before and I let it pass.

'Whatever do you find to talk about?' she asked me.

'It's hard,' I said. 'But I make most of it up. Street gossip. Stories of where I go and what I do. It passes the time.' I touched her arm. 'They need us there,' I said. 'To prove they've not been forgotten. You deserve a drink. We'll get one on the ferry.'

Once boarded, I bought her a stiff whisky, and one for myself. We had earned it, both of us. She for her silence, and me for the promise I would not fulfil. Once home, I went straight to our bedroom. I had been tempted before, but only vaguely for I knew that to examine Donald's clothes was an invasion.

We have two wardrobes in our bedroom, one on each side of the fireplace. I knew someone who worked in a charity shop where there were rails of men's suits. She told me they called them the morgue. The boys had urged me to give his clothes away, but that would have been as good as burying him and my Donald was going to get parole and we would be going to the sea together. He was going to need his clothes. All of them. This thought facilitated my opening. I could check what items I needed to take to the dry-cleaner's or the laundry.

The wardrobe released a musty smell and underlined the need for its airing. I felt a little better. He did not have many clothes, my Donald, but those he had were carefully looked after. Each of his three suits was over-hung with a plastic wrapper, already shrouded. I had in mind to go through the pockets. After all, if I was sending them to the cleaners, I needed to make sure that the pockets were empty. So I went through all of them, the jackets, the trousers, the waistcoats, and I found nothing. His shoes, scarves and gloves were on the top shelf. I had little hope of finding anything helpful among them. Nevertheless, I included them in my search. I stood on a chair to reach them comfortably, and suddenly I was overcome by a feeling of such despair and unhappiness. I think it was the sight of the empty shoes that sparked it off. Especially the empty sandals that he had worn on Margate beach. I started to cry, wail almost, so profound was my misery. I got down from the chair and sat on my bed and tried to calm myself. I can't go on like this, I thought. I have to believe that he is innocent. Truly, truly believe, or else I must bury him for good and all. But first I had to complete my search.

Once more I stood on the chair and examined the contents of the shelf. And found nothing. As I was tidying up the items I had disturbed, my fingers touched something solid. Whatever it was, was at the back of the shelf and covered with a cap and straw hat. Another Margate memory. I drew it out from beneath its camouflage. I knew it was evidence of a kind. I simply felt it in my bones. It was a box. Brown and of light weight. I held it carefully and laid it on my bed. There was no label on it of any kind, and I felt intuitively that it was just one more 'unmentionable' that I had to take to Parkhurst along with Emma, the boys, Devon, the wooden leg and the strange receipt for ashes. The box was not sealed and was easily opened. I was fearful of looking inside, so I turned my face away and felt its contents. It was a china vase of sorts, and it felt benign. It was possibly a present that Donald had bought for me and was putting aside until my birthday, along with a bunch of flowers that he would buy on the day. So I had no trouble in drawing it out of the box and turning my face to view it. I was disappointed. It was indeed a vase, but of a dull brown colour, worthy only of a bunch of weeds. The vase itself was covered, so I still had hopes that there was a birthday present inside. I took off the cover and on its inside I found its only label. 'Derek' it said – that was all. I dared to look inside the vase, and at least one of my 'unmentionables' was solved. The container was full of ashes. Presumably Derek's ashes, whoever Derek was. The plot thickens, I thought, and I don't know why, because I never knew the plot when it was thin. In fact, I didn't know anything about anything. On my next visit, I would have to ask Donald about Derek. I would spare him Emma; I would spare him the boys. And the wooden leg. But not Derek. But how could I know about Derek without letting on that I had looked in his wardrobe? Donald would take a poor view of that. He would deduce that I was giving away his clothes and that I thought he was guilty and that he would never come out of prison. So Derek had to join the unmentionables. I put the cover back on to the vase, and the vase into its box and back in the wardrobe where I had found it. I must never open that wardrobe again. I must put Derek out of my mind.

I was hungry, and I decided to take myself out for supper. Since Donald's arrest, I had never been to a restaurant alone. I would test myself. But I was wary of self-assertion, recalling the trouble it had landed me in in Turkey. And again I felt myself blushing. I prayed that Donald would be free. And soon. I so needed someone to take care of me.

I found a newly opened restaurant not far from our house. It was small, with few tables, and only one was occupied. By a lone woman like myself, and that comforted me. It called itself a French restaurant, but I was indifferent to its cuisine. I was simply hungry. I ordered a steak and french fries, together with a side salad. I enjoyed my meal, and as my hunger abated 'Derek' slipped from my mind. I knew he would be my waking thought, but I would deal with that in the morning. Or not deal with it, just as I didn't deal with anything else. Closing one's eyes, turning one's back, stuffing one's ears, all these manoeuvres are in themselves a method of dealing. It was the method that I had chosen. In that way, I could survive Donald's incarceration. In that way, I might even find a life of my own.

THE DIARY

NINE DOWN. NONE TO GO.

That's right. None to go. It's over.

It's early evening. Verry and the boys have gone to the pictures. And I have reached that state of elation that the crusade promised me. I am at peace at last. I am avenged, at peace. And, above all, innocent. Later on, I shall take his ashes to the common and scatter them there. On the rise where we used to fly our kites. Then it will all be over.

It was easy, this last one. Because I knew where I was going and what I was going to say. I would be free of gloves or any disguise. And I cared not about witnesses. I was excited. I was in sight of the mountain top, and all scruples had melted on my way. A strong sense of righteousness fuelled my every step to her door. My hands were clean, as was my conscience. I was high on innocence.

She only lives around the corner. When I bought our house, its location was a deliberate choice. I wanted to keep an eye on her. And I did, over the years. I watched her comings and goings. I viewed her frequent change of partners. She is a fickle woman. I know the inside of her house as well as I know my own. At least the ground floor. The hall, the kitchen and the consulting room. I learned it well from one who had been there, and who sadly knew it intimately.

I put on my best suit. The last station of my crusade I regarded as a ceremony and I dressed accordingly. From my constant observations I knew that she was at home at five o'clock. And alone. So that was the time, the killing-time of five in the afternoon, that I chose to make my call.

It took me only a few minutes to reach her house. I was calm. I rang the bell and, as I expected, Miss Robinson herself answered the door.

'Yes?' she asked.

A well of burning hatred overcame me, and I put my foot in the door. She could not escape me and she paled.

'What do you want?' she said.

'I need to speak to you,' I said. By now I was inside the house, and I shut the door behind me. She reached for the phone on the hall table. But I slapped her hand and pulled the instrument out of its socket. Terror creased her face, and I knew that her bowels were melting.

'We need to talk,' I said. I pushed her into her consulting room that was off the hall. 'Sit down,' I ordered. 'This may take a little while.'

She sat in the chair and her hand darted once again to the desk phone. I wrenched it from her. I was angry. I pulled the instrument off the desk, and flung it with all my force to the floor.

'You have no escape,' I told her. 'You just sit there like a good woman and listen to what I have to say.'

She was trembling. I took my last guitar string out of my pocket, and laid it on the desk. And then she realised who I was, and what I had come to do. She started to cry, but I was unmoved.

'My name is Dorricks,' I told her. 'Does that ring a bell?' She shook her head. Words had fled from her in fear.

'How about Derek Dorricks?' The name broke in my throat.

Again she shook her head.

'He was your patient,' I said. 'For nine solid years. Three times a week. I'm surprised you don't remember him.'

Another shake of the head.

'You killed him,' I said. Then I had to pause. I felt hot
tears burning my cheeks. I have not cried for many years.
Except inside myself. And that often enough. It was a relief
of sorts, and I made no move to stem them. 'Derek was a
manic-depressive,' I said. 'His GP recommended you. He
suggested a preliminary investigation. As it turned out, it
was not preliminary at all. It lasted for all of one thousand,
four hundred and four hours. It took you all that time to
discover or, rather, admit, that you could not help him. You
kept him by you for nine years since you needed him as
much as he needed you. Let me tell you about Derek,' I said.
That too would be a relief, I thought. Since his death, I'd
spoken about him to nobody. Except myself, and that,
endlessly over the years. 'He was a musician,' I said. 'A
guitarist, and a very talented one. The instrument was his
passion. That and the kites we flew together on the common.
He was a classical guitarist and he practised every day. He
studied at the Academy, and his teachers envisaged a fine
future for him. Then, when he was about eighteen, he sank
into a deep depression. And that was when he was sent to
you. But despite his condition, he never gave up on his practising. Every day he played as if the devil possessed him.
But he was playing badly. He was simply out of control. It
was then that you suggested, in your infinite wisdom, that
he put the guitar away. He trusted you. He loved you almost.
He talked about you all the time. And he listened to you.
On your orders, the guitar went back into its case. And a
major breakdown began. He was now in his fourth year of
your so-called therapy, and there was no sign of improve-
ment. And still he trusted you, with a pathetic three-times-
a-week trust that could not be shaken. I forced him to go

back to his doctor, who prescribed anti-depressants. But Derek would have none of it. You had told him that you viewed pills with contempt, and he was not going to let you down. Those pills might have saved him. I have known others whom they have saved. But you needed Derek by you. You would not let him go. Until the last year of your treatment. I found out that after many years of lonely living, you had at last found yourself a partner. Your need for Derek slowly evaporated. You yourself began to suggest pills. And you had the gall to claim that he had needed nine years of your counselling to prepare him for medication. For Derek it was the end of all his trust. He came home broken. That night, I couldn't find him in the house. I knew he hadn't gone out. Apart from your counselling, he rarely went out of doors. I looked for him all over. But I couldn't find him. Then I heard a noise that I traced to the attic. I rushed up the stairs and opened the door.'

I had to pause again. All that imaging I had done over the years, in spells of doubts and uncertainties, in moments of scruple, all that imaging now crystallised into woundingly sharp focus. It was as if I had discovered him only moments before. And I had to describe it in detail. Miss Robinson needed to know what she had done.

'Derek was hanging there,' I sobbed. 'From the ceiling. The stool he had used for his hanging had tipped over. That must have been the noise I heard from downstairs. I rushed to him in a frenzy and I cut him down. But it was too late. He was gone. He was twenty-eight years old.'

I had to pause once more as I saw the shattered guitar beside him. Then I described it to her, piece by broken piece. I looked at her for a while. I needed the silence. Then she dared to look at me and at last she found words.

'Please don't hurt me,' she managed to say.

There was no 'sorry', no remorse, no sympathy. Just a selfish egomaniac plea for her own survival.

I needed a little more silence before I could finish my story. I had to tell her why I had come. Why I had killed nine people, one for every year of her destruction. Why I had to avenge Derek's death, and find my own peace. I took a deep breath.

'Derek Dorricks was my brother,' I said. 'My twin. He was part of myself, and I of him. And we loved each other. You killed him,' I said, 'and you left me with a semi-life. I half live, I half work, I barely half love. And for all that, I'm going to kill you.'

I picked up the string and I moved behind her. I took my gloveless, joyful time. I circled the string gently around her neck as if I was fastening a delicate necklace. Then I pulled with a strength I did not know I possessed. I listened to her gurgles, and they were like music. I watched her die with infinite pleasure and then I pushed her limp and lifeless body off the chair. I heard myself laughing, and I saw my feet dancing as I moved towards the door. Once outside, I broke into a jig, and I danced my laughing way down the drive. There were people outside and they were staring at me. They must have thought I was mad. And in a way, I was. Mad with joy and fulfilment. I danced all the way home. I noticed that one of the spectators was following me and he stood outside my house, watching me as I jigged through my front door. I gave a thought to Wilkins. His hour had most certainly arrived.

I am calmer now. And at peace. I am writing the last words of my diary, and then I shall burn it for no one must ever know the cause of my crusade. It's getting dark. Verry and the boys will soon be home.

There is a knocking on the door. Not Verry. She has a key. I think they have come for me. But one more sentence before the fire. And then I shall be ready. So I write.

As God is my judge, I am innocent. History will absolve me.

Detective Inspector Evans was just about to leave his office when his phone rang. The desk clerk put through the call. 'He wants to speak to the chief,' he said. 'He won't tell me why.'

'Put him through,' Evans said.

'My wife has been murdered,' a voice screamed.

'Where are you?' Evans asked.

'Twelve, Wyndham Drive.'

'Stay there and don't touch anything. We'll be over right away.'

It was his first murder investigation since his promotion. He was nervous, and he wished Wilkins was by his side. But he knew the form, and he gathered together the crew he would need. The pathologist, the photographer and the print merchants. Together they drove to Wyndham Drive.

A small crowd had already gathered outside. They had heard the husband screaming as he ran from the house, anxious to tell the street of his loss. He was crazy with grief. Evans led his team inside, and formal investigations began. His heart had already missed a beat when he noticed a guitar string around the woman's neck.

'What did your wife do?' he asked, well knowing the answer.

'She was a psychotherapist,' the man said. 'And a very good one,' he sobbed.

Evans found an empty corner and phoned Wilkins.

His wife answered the phone. 'He's in the bath,' she said.

'Get him out,' Evans said. 'It's urgent.'

He waited and tried to be patient. He was excited. He had a feeling that they had run their quarry to ground. At last Wilkins came to the phone.

'He's done it again, sir,' Evans said. 'Fingerprints galore. And witnesses too, I gather. This is one for you.' He gave Wilkins the address and told him to hurry. Then he returned to the scene of the crime.

The pathologist gave his usual report. Cause of death, which was patently obvious. He added the time. The woman had been dead for about two hours. Wilkins arrived as he was pronouncing his verdict.

'What have we here?' he asked. 'Any sign of a break-in?' He hoped not. That would not be the pattern. In all his investigations, it seemed that the killer had been invited inside the house.

'No,' one of the crew said. 'But there's no shortage of fingerprints. They're everywhere.'

'Good,' Wilkins said. 'And what about witnesses?'

'There are three outside,' Evans whispered in Wilkins' ear. 'One especially. He saw a man leaving the house at about the right time. I've questioned him already, if you don't mind.'

'Why should I mind?' Wilkins asked. 'It's your case.'

'Yours too.' Evans smiled.

'I'm grateful,' Wilkins said. 'Who is this man?'

'A neighbour. And he's got quite a story.'

'Bring him inside,' Wilkins said. 'I'll find an empty space.'

The witness was anxious to be questioned once again. He said his name was Brian Telson, and he lived directly opposite the house. He was coming home from work and he noticed a man coming out of Miss Robinson's house.

'You couldn't miss him,' he said, 'because he was dancing a jig in the driveway. Throwing up his arms and laughing as if he'd pulled something off. Some business deal, maybe. Something like that. His face was familiar. I thought he lived round about. I was right too because I followed him. I didn't have to go far. He was dancing all the way and I saw him go into three, Founders Road, still laughing and dancing as he let himself into the house.

Wilkins made a note of the address. The witness was promising. Other witnesses were eager to come forward. One of them knew the man by sight, he said. Saw him often in the High Street. Had seen him ring Miss Robinson's bell round about five o'clock. Both witnesses were asked to describe the man. Separately. And both accounts tallied.

Wilkins felt he was entitled to hope. There was nothing to stop him going to the address straight away, simply to eliminate the man from their inquiries. Or that's what he'd say on the man's doorstep: a polite 'sorry to trouble you' visit. He waited for the investigation to be completed, then he told Evans to order the body to be taken away. He left a policeman with the bereaved widower, though there were enough ready neighbours at his side. He sent the crew back to the station, then he and Evans went to Founders Road.

He rang the bell and waited. He knew someone was at home because there were lights on in the house, and a small flicker of fire in the front-room grate. The longer he waited, the more his hopes were raised. Delay was suspicious. The man was perhaps hiding something. The flicker of flame died out, and Wilkins again rang the bell. He wished he knew his name. At last they heard footsteps behind the door. Perhaps they were dancing steps, Evans thought, still celebrating a supposed triumph.

A man answered the door, with a smile. Wilkins stared at him. The face was vaguely familiar, and he associated it with a pleasant occasion. His hopes were dashed once more.

'Detective Inspector Wilkins,' the man said. 'How good to meet you again.'

Wilkins hesitated.

'Dorricks. Donald Dorricks.' The man jogged his memory. 'Don't you remember? We had dinner together at the Manor House in Kent. The four of us. Your wife and mine. Now what can I do for you?'

Wilkins felt a fool. He'd been led up the garden path on this one. There was no way this Mr Dorricks was a killer. But he had to say something. 'There's been a murder committed not far from here. We're just making inquiries. Forgive me, Mr Dorricks, but we have to ask you where you were round about five o'clock this afternoon.'

'I was at Miss Robinson's house,' he said. 'Round the corner.'

Wilkins lost his voice and it was Evans who had to continue. 'Miss Robinson was murdered,' he said.

'I know,' Mr Dorricks said. 'I killed her.'

Wilkins had had enough. 'Please do not waste our time,' he said.

'I'm not,' Mr Dorricks told him. 'I'm telling you the truth. I killed her. Round about six o'clock. Maybe earlier.'

Wilkins marvelled at the man's composure. Or perhaps he was simply a lunatic.

'Out of interest,' Wilkins was friendly, 'how did you kill her?'

'Garrotted,' Mr Dorricks said. 'With a guitar string.

Like all the others, *including* Mademoiselle Lacroix in Paris.'

Evans unclasped the handcuffs from his belt. He didn't expect their man to make a run for it. Indeed, he seemed almost willing to accompany them to the station, for he held out his hands for the cuffing.

'Donald Dorricks,' he said. 'I am arresting you on suspicion of the murder of Adèle Robinson.' Then he read him his rights.

'May I get my coat?' Dorricks asked.

Evans followed him into the hall, and waited while he put his coat on. Then he led him to the car and bundled him inside. Wilkins did not encourage any more talk during the ride. The man had said enough. He just prayed that it was all true.

At the station, there was the usual routine of formalities, then Dorricks was taken to the interview room. He asked politely for a cup of tea, and politely it was given to him. He sat facing the detectives and said, 'I'll help you all I can.'

He didn't wait for questions. He knew what they would ask, and he simply volunteered the answers.

'Yes,' he said. 'I killed them. And all in the same way. I killed Harry Winston, and likewise Angela Mayling. Bronwen Hughes was the next on my list and then Alistair Morris. Dear Mademoiselle Lacroix followed, and then Dr James Fortescue. Mrs Stephens from Canterbury was next on my list. And then there was that poor Mr Quick who was only a dentist. My mistake, I confess. But at least I didn't count him in my crusade. That made seven altogether, and I needed nine. I was sorry about Miss Brown, but I had no choice. Then there was Miss

Robinson this afternoon. The last. And now I don't need any more.'

'What does "need" mean?' Wilkins asked. 'And why nine?'

'That is my concern,' Dorricks said, and it was clear he would say no more.

'But why *any* murder?' Wilkins persisted. 'Why at all?'

'It was my crusade,' Dorricks said with a little pride. 'My mission. The killings were a protest against evil. That is all I have to say.'

The interview terminated. They had had enough. Dorricks was taken to the cells.

'Do you believe him, sir?' Evans asked, when they were alone.

'I'm afraid I do,' Wilkins said. 'And I'm also delighted, but I don't understand it at all. The man *is* telling the truth. Of that there's no doubt. Thank you for calling me in,' he said. 'I shall feel better now sitting at my desk. I'll rest easy.

Mary was waiting for his return. And he had a tale to tell. He rehearsed it on the way home. 'You remember that nice couple we met at the Manor House? The Dorricks? The ones you wanted to stay in contact with? Well it seems that that nice Mr Dorricks turns out to be our killer. And, moreover, he's confessed.' But he told her nothing of the sort. Such a report would have diminished her. They'd arrested a man on suspicion. That's all that he gave her. She could come with him to court in the morning to hear the charge. He couldn't believe his luck. He had no doubt that Dorricks was guilty. But he sensed he was more than that.

'What kind of a man is he?' Mary asked.

'Bananas,' he said, and he had already begun to pity him. Miss Robinson's was a funeral he wouldn't have to attend. The stranger was in custody.

It's me again. Don't bother with the name. Nor where the accent should lie. It doesn't matter any more. I don't care how it's pronounced. In fact, I don't care if it's never pronounced at all.

I had a visitor this morning. Two in fact. It was only eight o'clock and I thought it might be the milkman. Through the glass of the front door I could see two figures. They looked like policemen. I opened the door and I saw that one of them was a woman. It was her presence that set my mind racing. For I knew that it was the man who had come with the news, and the woman had come with her consolation. 'May we come in?' he asked. Gently. So gently. And I knew. I knew. I let them into the kitchen. It was warm in there. Familiar and safe. I'd been drinking a cup of tea, and it was half-full on the table. I thought of offering them a cup. Anything to delay the news they had to tell me. Because I knew. I knew. 'I'm afraid we have sad news for you,' the policeman said. And the consolation moved towards me, putting its hand on my shoulder. 'Your husband has died,' the man said. 'How?' I asked. Though I knew. I knew. It couldn't have been a heart-attack. My Donald was in excellent health. And his blood-pressure was normal. Whatever they told me, I wouldn't believe. Because I knew. I knew. 'He was found early this morning. In the games room. He had hanged himself.' The consolation tightened its grip on my shoulder. 'Shall I make you some more tea?' it asked. I shook my head. I wouldn't believe it though I knew it was true. 'You have two sons,' the man

said. 'Would you like us to contact them?' 'No,' I said. 'I'll
do that. It's better I should do that. Much better. I'll do
that. Much better,' I kept saying. My mind was running
away from me, I knew. And I knew too that it would never
come back. 'Is there anything we can do for you?' the
consolation asked. I shook my head. I needed to finish my
tea and cook my breakfast. And carry on as if they had
never been. 'Please go,' I said. 'We'll be in touch about the
burial arrangements,' the man said. 'Are you sure there's
nothing we can do for you?' the consolation said again.
'Please go,' I said. 'It's much better that you go. Much
better.'

I heard them close the front door, then I finished my
cup of tea and told myself that Donald was dead, that he
had hanged himself. That he had taken the 'why' of it all
to his grave. That made me wonder whether they would
bury him or burn him. And then I thought of those ashes
in the wardrobe. Derek's. Whoever he was. I knew I had
to scatter them. But where? Did Derek like the sea perhaps?
Or the open fields? I would scatter them on the common,
I thought. Donald would like that. He told me he used to
fly his kite there when he was a little boy. Perhaps Derek
would like that too. I shall do that first thing tomorrow.
Much better. Much better. I shall leave this house, I think.
I only held on to it because of Donald. So that he would
have a home to come back to. Now I can leave it with no
sense of betrayal. I have been liberated at last, and monumentally against my will. This is a freedom I did not seek,
and for a moment I envied Mrs Cox who was still confined.
I must ring the boys. I would rather not tell them face to
face. I would fear their expressions. The phone is better for
such people with such news. I shall do that when I've

finished my cup of tea. Much better. Much better. Then I might start clearing the house. I shall pack his clothes first, with no misgivings, and then I shall send them to Oxfam, where they can hang on the morgue rail. Then I'll clean up the house and put it on the market. But first, more tea. Much better. Much better.

I take out the Hoover and I welcome the noise. It drowns all those words that were spoken in the kitchen. I won't turn it off because I'm afraid of their echo. I let it run as I drink another cup of tea. Much better. Much better. Then I clean out the grate as the Hoover hums. I haven't lit a fire since my Donald was taken away, but it is still full of ashes. I don't like ashes. I hate ashes, and I go at that grate with venom. It seems like a lot of paper has been burnt there and I rake it out. There's one slither of white among the pile, a scrap that dodged the flames. I pick it out. Donald's handwriting. Just a bit of a line. 'I am innocent,' I read. 'History will absolve me.' I stare at it while the Hoover hums. And I'm able to weep at last. Much better. Much better. I read it over and over again. There is no 'why' in it. No clue. And I cannot wait for history. History can take a very, very long time. But I shall keep the scrap of paper, and if I have the opportunity to go to Donald's funeral, I shall bury it with him. In all his innocence, he shall lie with history. Until he is absolved.

Much better. Much better.